Mrs. Entwhistle and the Amish Inn

Doris Reidy

Additional Titles by Doris Reidy

Doris Reidy

Dedication

To my sister and brother-in-law, Margaret and Mervin Hostetler, who always welcome me home.

Acknowledgements

I was brought up in a community in which many Amish families lived. The children went to grade school with us "English" kids, and we were all best friends until they left formal learning behind at age 16. My sister and brother-in-law have lived in that same little spot on the globe all their lives, and are surrounded by Amish neighbors. Those neighbors shovel snow, carry in freshly-baked bread, and bring their children to help weed the flower-beds. A kinder, gentler, and more eccentric people than the Amish would be hard to find. For authentic, non-sensationalized information about their way of life, go to the website Amish Studies at the Young Center of Elizabethtown College.

Chapter One

The summer morning fell open before them like a ripe cantaloupe. Golden and green fields stretched to the horizon on either side of the bus. The sky was as round and blue as an overturned bowl. Outside, serenity reigned. Inside was a different matter.

"The wheels on the bus go round and round, round and round, round and round," Maxine sang.

"Stop that!" Mrs. Entwhistle clapped her hands over her ears. "Now you've got it in my head and I'll be hearing it all day."

"It's called an ear worm, and you're welcome," Maxine said, grinning.

Mrs. Entwhistle and Maxine were diligent about snagging the first seats in the tour bus. Mrs. Entwhistle needed to see the horizon. She hated to admit she got motion sickness, but it couldn't be denied. If she had a front row seat and kept her eyes straight ahead, she could manage. Some of the other passengers muttered about people who felt entitled to the best spots, and Mrs. Entwhistle felt bad about that, but she said, "Needs must when the devil drives."

"I wonder what that even means," Maxine mused.

"Don't know, but my mother always said it when she was pushed to extremes," Mrs. Entwhistle replied.

"Speaking of extremes, I've really got to go," Maxine whispered.

Mrs. Entwhistle craned her neck around for a perilous look backward. Her stomach immediately gave a warning lurch. Eyes front!

"I don't see anyone heading toward the restroom," Mrs. Entwhistle reported. "Go ahead."

"But I just saw Frank come out a few minutes ago."

They gazed at each other in mutual consternation. Frank's recent presence in the unisex bathroom was a serious deterrent.

"I've got disinfecting wipes," Mrs. Entwhistle said, reaching for her big tote bag.

"And I've got air freshener," Maxine said, patting her capacious purse. "But still..."

"I know. Do you think you can wait until we get to the hotel?"

"Maybe, if I sit very still," Maxine said.

They saw Frank's wife, Mary Alice, heading for the back of the bus.

"How does she live with that every day?" Maxine wondered out loud.

"Perhaps she's lost her sense of smell." Mrs. Entwhistle's nose wrinkled at the thought.

They laughed, but not too hard. Maxine couldn't afford it.

"So here we are," Maxine said, "one of us with a needy bladder and the other with carsickness. Tell me again why we're on a bus trip?"

"Cheer up, honey. We'll be there in a few minutes. See, there's the city limits sign: Seltzburg, An Amish Community. I guess I should feel like I'm coming home, even though I've never set foot here before."

Mrs. Entwhistle had distant ties to the region. Her grandfather on her mother's side had been brought up nearby in an Amish family. Mrs. Entwhistle had been indoctrinated from an early age on stories about Jonas Hershberger's courage, industry and kindness, and she loved to pass those stories along. Despite her resolution to not become one of those boring old people who repeats herself, she couldn't resist a good opening, and here one was.

"Jonas Hershberger," Mrs. Entwhistle told Maxine again, "left his home and family when he was sixteen and moved south. Just think, he didn't know anybody, English was his second language, and he had only an eighth-grade education. Can you imagine the courage and resourcefulness he must have had?"

Jonas prospered through hard work and frugality, opening a small repair shop and soon becoming the go-to guy for broken lawnmowers and washing machines back in the days when household items were repaired, not discarded. He married a Southern girl who shared his work ethic and careful way with money, and somehow they parlayed the little repair shop into a general store. Then they bought a couple acres of land just outside of town, raised goats and chickens, kept a cow for milk, and introduced several tow-headed, intelligent children to the world. One of them was Mrs. Entwhistle's mother.

Family folk lore celebrated the quick-witted ancestor who piled strength upon strength, becoming modestly rich while never quite losing the trace of Pennsylvania Dutch accent that made his j's into ch's and his w's into v's. "I chust thought if you vas going that vay anyhow..."

Mrs. Entwhistle's memories of her grandfather had faded to a comfortable sepia brightened now and then by the retelling of family stories. Until she got the letter.

~*~

Anna May's calloused bare feet hardly registered the feel of the splintery wooden floor. The deck outside the restaurant was in full sun and the patio umbrellas weren't much help against the heat. She hoped the sweat on her forehead wasn't about to drip on the customers.

"That's a BLT, egg salad on rye and a cheeseburger; all with iced tea," she said, writing rapidly on her pad.

Once she'd turned in this order, her shift was over. Pop would be waiting in the buggy. The horse would be standing patiently at the hitching rail, flicking his tail at the flies that literally bugged his days. Anna May sighed inwardly at the thought of the slow jog home, the smell of liver and onions that would be floating from the kitchen (because it was Tuesday), and the chores she'd toil at until dark.

As an Amish girl, working at a paying job in the community was a privilege extended to her only for the benefit of the family. Mom and Pop reminded her of that every time she handed over her paycheck, receiving only a small allowance in return. They could withdraw their permission any time. Then she'd be stuck on the farm all day, every day. The tourists who made up the restaurant's clientele could be annoying, but at least they were new faces. Anna May tried to tamp down the restlessness that made her toss in her bed at night.

School had been a wonderland for her. Text books the other kids found boring opened new worlds to her, and the library was a constant source of joy. She wasn't allowed to check out novels from the school library, but if she finished her schoolwork, she could spend the rest of study hall reading. She got through **Lorna Doone** and **Treasure Island** that way. Having to leave before she finished **David Copperfield** was a continuing sadness.

With her sixteenth birthday, the education compelled by the state ended. Amish kids didn't graduate from high school. High school was considered a bridge too far, a temptation too great. Maybe young people exposed to science and literature and trigonometry wouldn't want to return to the farm, to the Amish way of life. Worse yet, maybe raging teenage hormones would promote a romance with an English person – a non-Amish individual. That was something to be avoided at all costs.

Anna May knew all that, but on the eve of her sixteenth birthday, she approached her father. She had to at least try.

"Pop, do you think it might be possible for me to stay in school a little bit longer?" She'd clasped her hands together to stop their trembling.

"Why, Anna May, what would you do with all that book learning?" Pop smiled indulgently at his bright daughter. "You'll get married, have a houseful of children and be a good Amish mother like your Mom. You can read and figure better than most already. Any more learning would just make you discontented."

Too late, Anna May thought. She bowed her head in submission.

~*~

The tour bus disgorged its passengers at the hotel's front doors under a canopy displaying the sign, Seltzburg Inn. It was an imposing building for such a small town. Not even a town; a wide place in the road, really. But the Seltzburg Inn was within walking distance of the Seltzburg Flea Market, and it stayed solidly booked during the summer season. Town residents had quickly adjusted from living in a sleepy backwater to hustling for the tourist dollar.

Maxine quick-walked toward the bathroom while Mrs. Entwhistle scoped out the big hotel lobby. The space was filled with light and the staff seemed to wear perpetual smiles. There were huge blow-up photographs of Amish life, with the people seen only from the back, which fascinated Mrs. Entwhistle. As she worked her way down a corridor lined with pictures, Maxine rejoined her.

"Why don't the pictures show their faces?" Maxine asked.

"They never face the camera," Mrs. Entwhistle said. "There's a Bible verse forbidding graven images, and they believe that applies to photographs."

"So, no baby pictures? No wedding photos, or special occasion snapshots?"

"Nope."

"It seems disrespectful to picture them at all, then; it's like an ambush," Maxine said, and Mrs. Entwhistle agreed.

But they couldn't help enjoying the photos of an Amish blacksmith bent over the dinner-plate-sized hoof of a patient Belgian draft horse, and a trail of ducklings waddling behind a tiny boy in a straw hat. Another featured a dog riding high atop hay baling wagon. That made Mrs. Entwhistle miss her dog, Roger.

"I'm worried about Rog," she said to Maxine.

She'd said that at regular intervals since they'd left home. Usually, if she traveled and couldn't take him along, she left Roger with friends or hired someone she knew to stay at her house and look after him. But this time none of her friends were available, and she had to leave Roger at a kennel. True, it was his own vet's facility, where Roger had been so many times that it might have seemed like home to the old fellow. But still. A dog used to sleeping on his human's bed would have a hard time adjusting to life in a kennel. Mrs. Entwhistle had bought him a new bed to take along, and filled it with one of her old sweaters and a towel from home so he'd at least have the comfort of familiar smells.

"I hope the other dogs' barking isn't driving him crazy," she said.

"That's one good thing about being deaf," Maxine said. "I bet Roger can't even hear them."

That was a comforting thought, and Mrs. Entwhistle decided she'd go with it. There wasn't a thing she could do for Roger until she got home, anyway.

Maxine and Mrs. Entwhistle always packed light. No sense in taking a lot of clothes, they agreed. Sitting on the bus didn't call for high fashion, and besides, they were experts at mixing and matching. They picked up their two small bags from the pile of luggage dumped in the lobby by the bus driver and headed for their room. Once there, Maxine insisted on leaving the bags outside the door while she performed a reconnaissance.

She threw back the bedcovers and peeled the fitted sheet from the mattress. Illuminated by her phone's flashlight, she ran the edge of a credit card along the mattress seams. Nodding in satisfaction when she didn't find anything suspicious, she advanced to the bathroom, flung back the shower curtain, eyeballed the tile grout for mold, inspected the bathtub for stray hairs, flushed the toilet and shook out a bath towel.

"It's spotless," Maxine decreed.

"That's because they have Amish cleaners," Mrs. Entwhistle said. "Did you notice the woman pushing a cleaning cart in the hall just now?"

"I did. But I didn't know Amish women worked outside their homes."

"I didn't think so, either; apparently, times have changed."

"But isn't the whole point of being Amish making sure that you don't change with the times?" Maxine asked.

"Well, maybe not the whole point, but a big one, anyway. Young couples can't count on farming to make a living anymore, because the available farmland is pretty well taken. So some of the men work in trailer factories and some of the women and girls take service jobs. There's a big tourist industry here in the summer time. I imagine it put them outside their comfort zone at first, but they adapted. They had to."

"Surely they are capable of doing more than factory work," Maxine said. "Aren't any of them in professions? Teachers or doctors or something?"

"Oh, no doubt they could be, but without an education…" Mrs. Entwhistle's voice trailed off.

"But they must go to school. It's the law."

"You know, that law actually went to the Supreme Court in 1972. I looked it up. The court ruled that Amish are exempt from compulsory schooling after the eighth grade because of their religious beliefs. They can quit school then, and they do."

"But why?"

"The Amish believe their rural way of life only calls for the ability to read, write and do basic math.. Anything beyond that might tempt their kids to stray from Amish beliefs."

Maxine shook her head. "Well, I certainly respect

their religion, but it seems a shame to arbitrarily stop learning and experiencing the world at a certain age."

"The young people have one more option to sample what they call the English life. When they are in their mid to late teens, they can go on rumspringa."

"I watched a television show about that," Maxine said, pursing her lips disapprovingly. "There was a lot of drinking and drug-taking and car wrecks. Of course, that might have been exaggerated for the show."

"Maybe," Mrs. Entwhistle said. "But I think a fair amount of that does go on. The hope is that the kids will sow their wild oats and return to the Amish way of life. Most of them do."

"But some don't?"

"No. Some don't. My grandfather didn't. They call it 'going high,'— Jonas went high and left the Amish."

"My folks used his repair shop," Maxine said. "Mother always said the children, including your mother, were beautiful, with one blonder and prettier than the next. She claimed to be jealous."

"My mother was the youngest. Grandpa died when I was a child, but whenever I smell butterscotch, I think of him. He always had butterscotch candy in his pocket for me. I can't remember his face, but that smell takes me right back to him. Isn't it amazing the memories that scents trigger?"

"Not if you're Frank's wife," Maxine said. She didn't have to worry about laughing too hard now.

Chapter Two

It all started for Anna May the day she'd been cleaning the attic. It was the kind of sleety, windy weather that discouraged even Mom from her weekly window washing. Anna May wore her padded winter jacket and was still cold. She could see her breath as she swept the floor and rubbed the cloudy panes in the eaves window.

The old trunks that lined the walls exuded the dusty smell of old papers, a come-hither aroma for a reader. After her work was finished, she pulled forward the oldest and opened the lid. That's where she found the letters.

They fell from the folds of an ancient quilt when she lifted it from the trunk. The rusty metal clasp on the envelope broke in Anna May's fingers. Inside were papers fragile as an eyelash. Carefully, Anna May unfolded the first one.

Round, childlike handwriting, the ink faded to faintest lavender, filled the page. She carried it over to the light of the window.

Dear Pop,

How are you? I am fine. It is nice here; we don't hardly have no winter at all. Rains a lot, and the ground ain't good for crops because of rocks and clay soil. I got a shop now where I fix things.

Pop, I would like to come home for a visit. I know Mom ain't in good health, and I would sure like to see her ~~before she~~. I would not stay long, and you don't have to tell no one I am coming, nor that I was there. Let me know if I can come."

Your son,

Jonas

Dear Mom,

I won't come if it would cause trouble for you with the bishop. But if you would just see me for an hour. I wouldn't have to eat nothing, or sit at the table or see nobody else.

Your son,

Jonas

Dear Pop,

I hated to hear that Mom's gone. I wish I could have just seen her once more. I'm sorry.

Your son,

Jonas

That was the last letter. Anna May searched the trunk, but there were no more. Jonas had to be an ancestor; she'd seen his name written in the family Bible along with so many others. Now she was curious. She clattered down the attic stairs to find her mother.

"Who was Jonas Hershberger?" she asked, only to see her mother's face tighten.

"He was my great-grandfather," Mom said, with a warning look, "but we don't talk about him."

"I found some of his old letters in the attic," Anna May said, her curiosity overriding her good sense. "It sounded like he was under the miting. He wanted to come home, he said, to see his mother. That would have been your grandma. What happened?"

"He died to us, to our family," Mom said flatly. She turned her back and got busy at the stove.

That was the end of that subject, and Anna May knew better than to ask any more questions. She could piece it together for herself. Jonas had been shunned. He'd done the unforgiveable—left the farm, the family, the Amish—and he'd paid the price. Being under the miting, the shunning, meant he was no longer welcome in the Amish church and his family would not see him, would not eat with him, talk to him, or allow him in their homes. It was hard to think of a more hurtful interdiction for family-loving Amish people. And still, Jonas had had the courage to follow his own wishes. Anna May looked out the window thoughtfully.

~*~

Anna May was awakened by the sound of retching. Rising carefully so as not to wake her younger sister, she tiptoed to the window and lifted the edge of the plain green paper shade. There was her brother, Levi, on his hands and knees with his head in the hydrangea bush. Most surprisingly, Pop was bending over Levi, supporting his head as he heaved.

"Kutze alle," Pop murmured. "Get it all out. You'll be all right."

Anna May marveled at the patience in Pop's voice. He didn't sound a bit mad, and she'd have thought he'd be furious. Glancing at the wind-up alarm clock, she saw it was three a.m. Pop would have been rising for the day in another hour; he didn't take kindly to being cheated out of his sleep. And by a drunken son, yet. Anna May shook her head as she climbed back into bed. If it had been her, she'd have had to go out in the yard and cut a switch for Mom to use on her. Why did boys get away with such behavior?

When the alarm jarred her awake again at six o'clock, she remembered what she'd seen. Pulling her clothes on quickly, she went to Levi's room and pressed her ear to the door. No sounds issued from within. She turned the doorknob and stuck her head in.

"Lee?" she whispered.

There was a groan from the direction of the bed. "Go 'way, Ammay."

That Levi used her family nickname somehow melted the anger Anna May had been feeling. She ventured inside the door.

"Are you okay?" she asked.

"Feel like a horse kicked me," Levi muttered. "Go 'way."

So Anna May did, running down the stairs to the kitchen, already fragrant with the aromas of coffee and bacon.

"Mom! Did you know Levi -" she began.

"Yes, I know all about it," Mom said, cutting her off. "Sit down and eat your breakfast. I want you to weed the truck patch before you go to work today, so you'll have to get started early."

"But, Mom, Levi's sick. He said he feels like a horse kicked him."

"Well, it's his own fault, and we don't feel sorry

for him. He did it to himself." Mom's mouth was a thin line.

"Yeah, but why do boys get away with that stuff? If a girl did it, she'd get clobbered."

"Boys don't get in the family way," Mom said succinctly. "It ain't fair, but that's how the good Lord made us, so we have to accept it. And besides, some girls do run wild on rumspringa. I hope you won't be one of them."

"I don't even want to," Anna May said. "It don't look like much fun, if it's all that puking Levi was doing last night. But still..."

"Still, what?"

"Well, I'd still like to see more of the world, I guess."

"No good comes of it, Anna May, unless you count it good to make yourself so sick of something you don't want it anymore."

Anna May was quiet as she helped Mom feed the rest of the family and clean the kitchen. She headed out to the truck patch in the light of a sun-spangled morning, hardly noticing the red-winged blackbirds that flew aerial ballets over the fence posts. She bent to separate the weeds from the vegetables without conscious thought. She could weed blind-folded; she'd been doing it since she toddled at Mom's skirts.

There was a secret laying heavy on her heart. She hadn't accepted Mom's edict that the memory of

Jonas Hersherger was off-limits. She'd asked to leave the restaurant early one day and headed over to the library. There she'd asked the librarian to help her with some genealogy research.

There were few things Miss Pim liked better than research. She eagerly dropped what she was doing behind the reference desk, adjusted her computer screen so Anna May could also see it, and started tapping the keys.

Anna May was amazed at the information that could be called up with a few keystrokes. She saw a family tree with Jonas's family and their descendants. There was even an aerial picture of his little farm. It made him seem real somehow.

As she studied the names of Jonas's family, one name popped out at her. Cora Entwhistle, one of Jonas' granddaughters. She was the only close relation to Jonas still alive, and she was old now. She must have known him and could tell first-hand stories, but Anna May would have to hurry before there was a slash through her name on the tree.

"Could you look up Cora Entwhistle?" she asked Miss Pim.

And there it was, like magic, a short bio of one Cora Entwhistle, including her address. Anna May left the library telling herself she wasn't sure what she was going to do with the information she'd received, but deep down, she knew. The knowledge perched on her shoulders.

When she wrote the first letter, she gave her return address as that of the restaurant. Mom and Pop would not understand her urge to get in touch with a distant relative connected with the family reprobate. And since she was a girl, she'd be given no slack.

The connection was tenuous, like putting a note in a bottle and casting it out to sea. The old lady would probably not respond. Anna May didn't even know if she was still at that address. Maybe she'd died. It would probably come to nothing.

~*~

Dear Mrs. Entwhistle,

You don't know me, but I believe we are related. My name is Anna May Bontrager, and I am an Amish girl, age 18. The library lady helped me look up our family tree, and that's where I found you. I'm writing about Jonas Hershberger, your grandfather and my great-great grandfather.

I found some of Jonas' letters in a trunk in the attic. He was begging his father to let him come home to see his mother before she died, but I guess the answer was no. When I asked Mom about it, she got mad and said we don't talk about him. I think he was shunned by her family and the Amish community after he left the church. Isn't it wrong to keep shunning him after all these years?

I think I have a right to know more about him since he was my ancestor. He must have been very strong to leave everything he knew for a different life. What was he like? Was he a kind man? How did he look? Did you love him? Was he a good grandpa?

Anyway, if you have any stories about your grandfather and wouldn't mind sharing, I would love to hear them.

Your relative,

Anna May Bontrager

"If you have any stories about your grandfather...."

Mrs. Entwhistle laid Anna May's letter down and shook her head. Well, of course, she had stories, and there was nothing she liked better than sharing them. She remembered her mother telling endless tales as they sat on the porch shelling peas, or stringing beans, or peeling peaches. Those stories were precious; they had shaped her. Here was a stranger who claimed to be a relation asking for family lore. How could she not respond?

But there was more to the letter than a request for a stroll down memory lane. Mrs. Entwhistle was an expert at reading between the lines. This girl, this Anna May Bontrager, was on the cusp of something big in her life. Mrs. Entwhistle knew it without knowing how she knew.

How should she respond? She heard her mother's voice again, talking about her own father, Jonas Hershberger.

"He was a giant of a man. Six feet four, and strong! He used to say if you picked up a calf every day, in time you'd be able to pick up a full-grown cow, and I believed he could have. Once one of the mares dropped a foal out in the field. Or she tried to, anyway, but the baby wouldn't get born. The mare was about crazy with pain and kept pacing and whinnying. Dad went out there and coaxed that mama horse down on her side, and then he rolled up his shirt sleeve, lay down flat and stuck his arm 'way inside her. He found the baby's foot and pulled and pulled until finally the foal slid out on the ground. I can still hear the sploosh and see those spindly legs. Dad didn't mind that I watched, and he gave me a handful of straw and showed me how to wipe the foal down until the mare could get on her feet and tend to it."

Mrs. Entwhistle could still see her mother's eyes as she related that incident. "That's why I've always loved horses," her mother had continued. "It started with that baby. Dad let me name him, and I chose Pegasus because we'd studied about him in school. And when my birthday came, Dad put a ribbon around Pegasus's neck and led him right up to the kitchen steps.

'Here's your birthday present,' he said. Dad didn't talk much, but I could see what it meant to him. I had that horse until he finally died of old age. Dad was gone by then, too, and I felt like I'd lost him again when Pegasus died."

Mrs. Entwhistle wrote that story in a letter of reply to Anna May.

"Probably won't hear from her again," she said to Maxine. "She won't want to keep up a correspondence with an old lady."

But Anna May did. As the handwritten letters passed slowly back and forth via snail mail, Mrs. Entwhistle formed a mental picture of her correspondent. *She's smart and curious about the world outside her Amish community. If she were not Amish, she'd be one of those kids who spends a year with a European family as an exchange student, or gets a job as an au pair in Australia. For her, those options don't exist, so she's trying to create her own window on life.*

They exchanged news about what was going on in each of their lives, and gradually shared their thoughts about current events, deepening even more into philosophical discussions about human behavior. Mrs. Entwhistle looked forward to hearing from Anna May and spent some time composing her replies. Sometimes she almost forgot that she was corresponding with a teenager, and an Amish teenager at that.

One day a very different letter arrived. To Mrs. Entwhistle, it sounded like a cry from the heart.

"I have to get out of this place!" Anna May wrote. "I feel like I'm smothering. Not that I don't love

Mom and Pop and my brothers and sisters. I do. But, I don't know, I can't say it good, I just need more than the farm and church every other Sunday in somebody's buggy shed."

"What? Church in a shed?" Maxine interrupted, when Mrs. Entwhistle read her the letter.

"There are no Amish church buildings," Mrs. Entwhistle said. "They don't believe in spending money on buildings, I guess. Grandpa used to tell about the church wagon that contained benches and was pulled from house to house in the district. I think each family hosted once a year. The service was held in a barn or outbuilding big enough to hold a crowd of about 150 people. The preachers were laymen with no formal training in theology, and they spoke in a mix of German and Dutch, so it must have been hard to understand what was being said."

"Can you imagine? Did they have Sunday School?"

"Nope, and Grandpa said the service was three hours long, with everyone sitting on backless benches." Mrs. Entwhistle shook her head. "And the songs! He said it was like plain chant, sung without accompaniment, very slowly. One song might take fifteen minutes. But then they'd have a light meal. He said it would consist of things like coffee, bread, 'church spread,' which was a combination of peanut butter and marshmallow, jam, apple butter, red beets, pickles, cheese, and sometimes apple pie. I bet the menu hasn't changed much to this day. Then they'd socialize, and that was important. Life on an isolated farm with no radio, television, or newspaper would get a bit monotonous, don't you think?"

"How do they know what's going on in the world?" Maxine wondered.

"They don't."

Their heads nodded at the same moment. "Better off."

They turned back to Anna May's letter.

"I feel like I have to get away, maybe not forever, but just for a while, to see what the English world is like. But I don't want to go on rumspringa. My brother is on rumspringa, and he comes home drunk and sick. It doesn't look like fun. And last year a boy in our church died from a drug overdose.

"So I'm going to ask a big thing. Could I come visit you? I'd like to see the town where Jonas Hershberger lived after he left here. You actually knew him, so you could tell me first-hand stories. I wouldn't be a bother, I promise. I know how to work, and I'll do anything you need done inside the house or out. I can mow your yard, clean the attic, scrub whatever needs scrubbing, and cook your supper every night. You wouldn't need to entertain me. It would be enough for me just to be in a different place. If it's not too much to ask."

Mrs. Entwhistle laid the letter on the table, took off her glasses and rubbed her eyes. "Well, I don't know what to say."

"She sounds like a sweet girl, but you wouldn't want to get crossways with her folks," Maxine said. "And what have I heard about some kind of shunning?"

"They used to do that," Mrs. Entwhistle said. "I don't know how common it is these days, but in the past, if an Amish person did something the church thought was really bad, like leave the faith, they would shun him. They called it the miting. Anna May told me she found letters in which Jonas asked permission to see his mother before she died, but he apparently didn't get it. Under the rules of the miting, he couldn't be received in his family home or be acknowledged or even spoken to."

"Wow. That seems harsh," Maxine said.

"Yes. Maybe it's a thing of the past now. I hope so."

"So what are you going to tell Anna May?" Maxine asked.

Mrs. Entwhistle sighed. "What do you think I should do?"

"Ordinarily, I'd say you should welcome her. She's a young person asking for your help in finding her way in life. But this situation isn't ordinary."

"I may be too old to take on such a task," Mrs. Entwhistle said.

Maxine laughed. "I know better than to agree. If I say anything that sounds at all like a double-dog dare, that's exactly what you'll do. But think about it, Cora. Anna May might be related to you, but the connection is so distant it hardly counts. She's a teenager. Once she gets away from home, anything could happen. Maybe it would be better to steer clear of this one. Really, it's not your problem."

Mrs. Entwhistle knew Maxine was talking sense. They'd both lived long enough to spot trouble when it stuck its face around the corner. But there was something about Anna May's request that kept poking at her.

"Jonas was my grandfather, and even though his relationship with Anna May is down the ladder in the great-great category, we come from the same stock. Grandpa had to overcome a lot of hardships when he left the Amish, and he often spoke of the people who welcomed and helped him. He always said kindness, when given away, keeps coming back."

"Is this something you feel you have to do?" Maxine asked.

"Maybe. It keeps tugging at me. After all, there are people who donate a kidney to a stranger, and here's me, reluctant to extend hospitality to a distant relation because it might be inconvenient."

Maxine watched silently as Mrs. Entwhistle got up and began to vigorously wipe down the countertops. She grabbed the throw rug in front of the sink, took it to the backdoor and shook it within an inch of its life. Then, relieved of some inner tension, she sat back down at the table.

"Before I decide what to do, I need more information. I want to know more about this child and where she comes from."

"How do you propose to find out?"

"What do you think about taking a little trip, Max?"

"Driving? I don't know about that."

"Not driving. I read about a bus trip that goes through Tennessee, Kentucky and Indiana, ending up in Seltzburg where there's some kind of famous flea market."

"Flea market? You? You start tapping your foot in the check-out line at the Piggly Wiggly. I don't see you wandering around a flea market."

"We wouldn't actually have to go to the flea market," Mrs. Entwhistle said patiently. "But Seltzburg is where Anna May lives. We could meet her, maybe visit with her parents and see their farm. I believe it'd give me a much better feel for what to do. And if I decide not to have her visit, well, we've had a little outing and seen some more of the country. We haven't gone anywhere since we got back from our trip on Route 66."

She didn't have to work too hard to convince Maxine, who was always up for an adventure. And so they eventually found themselves in a spotless room at the Seltzburg Inn, sitting on the edges of their beds, plotting their next move.

Chapter Three

"Can we call an Uber?" Maxine wondered out loud. She thumbed through the stack of brochures provided by the inn.

"I doubt it," Mrs. Entwhistle said. "I don't think Uber has penetrated this far yet."

"Well, then how are we going to get to the Bontrager farm?" Maxine asked. "How will we know where to find it? You said Anna May had you send your letters to a café in town, so we don't even have her home address."

"Yes, and that bothers me. Obviously, she didn't want her parents to know about our correspondence. I don't like being part of something sneaky."

"But you also don't want to get your little friend in trouble at home."

This trip was challenging them in ways they'd not anticipated. They sat silently, minds churning.

"I could eat," Maxine finally said.

"Me, too. Let's see if we can find that café where Anna May works. Even if she's not there today, I could inquire very tactfully about her."

Maxine cocked an eyebrow at the idea of Mrs. Entwhistle's tactfulness, but she didn't say anything. She offered no better suggestion. They stopped at the front desk to ask how long a walk it was to Main Street.

"Why, just, oh, maybe half a mile," the young desk clerk said uncertainly. "But it's a real busy road and there are no sidewalks. People around here don't really walk much. You could take the buggy ride, though."

They followed his pointing finger to the wall of windows at the front of the lobby and saw a black Amish buggy outside. It was hitched to a shining chestnut mare, and the driver wore black Amish garb. The horse and driver had identical expressions of patient boredom.

"It costs five dollars," the clerk said warningly. "Each." He wanted to be sure there were no unpleasant surprises on his watch.

"Oh, let's do it, Cora!"

Mrs. Entwhistle smiled at her friend's enthusiasm. That was one of the best things about Maxine. She was always open to trying something new. Sometimes that led to a certain gullibility that Mrs. Entwhistle deplored, but an adventurous spirit was a good thing. Especially for older ladies.

"Sure, why not?" she said, and they approached the horse and buggy.

Maxine stopped to stroke the horse's velvety nose and was rewarded by a snort and a nervous shuffling of hooves.

"She ain't used to being off the farm," the driver said. "She's a real good buggy horse, just young yet. This is her first day in town."

"Our first day in town as well," Mrs. Entwhistle said. "Could we hire a ride to Main Street?"

The café where Anna May worked was called the Guten Essen. It perched almost on the narrow sidewalk of Seltzberg's Main Street, a perfect location for reeling in unwary passersby with tempting aromas. The oil-cloth covered tables were mostly empty in mid-afternoon, except for one family with several children who were quietly eating ice cream cones. Mrs. Entwhistle and Maxine sat by the window and waited for the lone Amish waitress to make her way over to them.

"Yah? What can I get you?" she asked. Her hair was braided close to her head and tucked under an immaculate white head covering. A long, dark dress swished around her bare feet.

Maxine gave herself a little shake and averted her eyes from the naked toes. "Uh, just a cup of tea, please," she said. "And please be sure to make it with boiling water."

"Same for me," Mrs. Entwhistle said. "Earl Grey, if you have it. Is Anna May Bontrager working today?"

"Anna May? She's not coming in until four. Do you know her?" The waitress couldn't conceal her curiosity.

"Oh, not really. She may be a very distant relative. I just thought I'd say hello, that's all." Mrs. Entwhistle was off-hand. She didn't want to crank up the gossip mill.

After they'd drunk their tea, Mrs. Entwhistle and Maxine poked around among the many shops lining Main Street, killing time until four. Little frame houses that once were family homes now contained boutiques selling every touristy object that could possibly be connected to the Amish, and quite a few that could not. They inspected Amish faceless dolls, Amish postcards, Amish quilts, Amish apple butter, Amish bonnets, Amish sayings embroidered into samplers. In due time, Mrs. Entwhistle's patience ran out.

"For heaven's sake!" she snapped in the fifth store. "We don't want any of this stuff. C'mon, Max."

She led the way back onto the sidewalk, taking care not to stomp angrily. It wasn't the shopkeeper's fault she had no tolerance for kitsch.

A sign on the door of a large new building announced *Yoder Popcorn Museum. Free Popcorn!* "Here we go, Max, this is more like it," Mrs. Entwhistle said, leading the way into the tantalizing perfume of buttered popcorn. Fortified with paper bags of freshly popped corn, they inspected displays illustrating the planting, harvesting and popping of corn.

"Not exactly riveting," Maxine whispered.

"No, but the popcorn's good," Mrs. Entwhistle replied, pausing respectfully before an enormous green John Deere tractor that took up a good portion of the shop's square footage.

Finally, it was four o'clock and they could go back to Guten Essen and seek out Anna May. Mrs. Entwhistle recognized her immediately— something about the slant of her eyes and the way she carried her head stirred a memory of Grandpa Hershberger. The girl was wearing a dark brown dress with a high neck, long sleeves and a hem just above her ankles. Her shining blond hair was pinned up in braids and covered with a pleated white head covering. She looked as clean and wholesome as fresh milk in a glass bottle.

"Anna May? I'm Cora Entwhistle. It's nice to finally meet you."

Anna May's eyes widened. "Why, I didn't know

you'd come!" she said. "I never expected...I'm so glad to finally meet you, too. Are you here just for me?"

"We came on the tour bus," Mrs. Entwhistle said. "But you were the reason we got on that bus. Is there a time when we can talk?"

Anna May glanced at the few people seated in the café. "It's not busy now, but I'm supposed to be in the kitchen helping with supper prep. I get off at eight, and my brother is going to pick me up in the buggy. Maybe I could get him to bring me to your hotel. Are you staying at the Inn?"

"That's right. Will your brother mind waiting for you?"

"No, I'll give him a couple of dollars for the arcade games. He's not supposed to play them, none of us are, but he does it every chance he gets. That'll keep him occupied for a while. We'll tell our folks we're late because we, uh, we stopped to wade in the creek."

"I don't like to be part of a lie to your parents," Mrs. Entwhistle said sternly.

"You won't be. We really will stop at the creek on our way home so our feet will be wet." Anna May had an appealing set of dimples and they deepened now as she grinned.

Mrs. Entwhistle shrugged. "Okay, then. We'll be in the lobby at eight."

~*~

"I see you have shoes on now," Maxine said, when Anna May approached them in the Inn.

"Yah, the restaurant makes us go barefoot for the tourists. Local color, they call it. I do go barefoot at home, but I wouldn't do it in town. Well, splinters, for one thing. But the tourists get a kick out of it, so the owner said we have to do it. Isn't very sanitary, is it?" Those dimples again.

"Anna May, tell me why you want to come visit," Mrs. Entwhistle said, wasting no time in getting straight to the point.

Anna May reddened. "It was easier to ask in a letter. It's too much, isn't it? You don't want an Amish teenager hanging around your house. I'm sorry, I should have thought it through better."

"No, no, that's not the case at all. If it was, I'd just say no. I'd actually love for you to visit, but I need to know your folks are okay with it, and that you're not running away from anything here that you should be dealing with. Like a romance gone bad?"

"Oh, not that!" Anna May said, growing even redder. "I don't have a boyfriend. Well, just Abe, but not even, if you know what I mean. He's, well, I've known him since we were babies. He's a friend. Maybe our folks hope we'll get together some day, but we feel more like brother and sister. No, I just wish I could be in a place that wasn't Amish. Not that I don't love my family and all."

Anna May stopped, emotional distress written on her face. Mrs. Entwhistle looked off in the distance to give her time to collect herself. Maxine smiled sympathetically and patted the girl's knee. They waited.

"I thought if I could go where my ancestor went when he left the Amish, maybe I'd feel like I belonged there a little bit and it wouldn't be quite so scary to be out in the world." Anna May shrugged. "I guess that's stupid."

"So you want to push yourself out of your comfort zone," Mrs. Entwhistle said. "Why?"

"It's not enough!" Anna May burst out. "Here just isn't enough. I sit in a tiny corner of the world and wonder what else is out there. I want to see more and know more and do more."

"We don't exactly live in Gotham City," Maxine said, shaking her head at Anna May's puzzled look. "Never mind. What I mean is, we live in a small town. If you want bright lights and a lot going on, you'll be disappointed."

"Bright lights would be even scarier," Anna May said, smiling.

Just then a boy with hair so blond it looked white approached shyly. He ducked his head and tugged on Anna May's dress.

"Did you run out of money?" she asked, detaching his fingers. "Jacob, meet Mrs. Entwhistle and Mrs.?"

"Gober," Maxine supplied.

Jacob nodded, too shy to look up. "Ammay, ve hame gae?"

"Yah, sure, we should be going." Anna May said.

"When would be a good time for us to come to the farm and meet your parents?" Mrs. Entwhistle asked.

Both Jacob's and Anna May's eyes grew round. "Uh, do you think...?" Anna May began.

"It's the only way," Mrs. Entwhistle interrupted her firmly. "I'm a mother myself, and I won't have another mother worried about where her daughter is. Just in case you were thinking about sneaking off."

Anna May blushed again. Clearly, she had been thinking just that. "Tomorrow is Sunday," she said, "but it's not church Sunday, so we'll be at home. But maybe I should..."

"Tomorrow it is. Please tell your parents to expect us."

Chapter Four

Anna May's thoughts churned as she and Jacob clip-clopped home behind the buggy horse, Bess. The big trucks zoomed by too close for either comfort or safety, but she hardly heard them. The horse pricked her ears, but never missed a step in her steady trot along the buggy lane that flanked the road. Bess had been born with nerves of steel and a natural inclination to pull a buggy, which was fortunate because she was getting little guidance from the reins that lay limp in Anna May's hands.

"Sis, what did that lady mean about coming to see Mom and Pop tomorrow?" Jacob asked.

"Never mind, Jake, it's just something...well, I have to talk to them about an idea I had."

"You ain't going on rumspringa, are you?"

"No, it's not like that. I might just go on a visit."

"But why, Ammay? Why don't you stay home?"

"That's all I've ever done," Anna May began, but the puzzled look on her brother's face stopped her words. "Hey, don't worry about it. Mom and Pop will probably say no, and that will be that."

"You wouldn't run away, would you?" Jacob's voice cracked a little with worry. He was twelve, and he was embarrassed when that happened.

"No, of course not," Anna May replied, but her words didn't sound convincing even to her.

She waited until after supper when the preparations for tomorrow's breakfast had been made, and the kitchen was once again shining clean. Mom and Pop went out to the grape arbor together, and the sound of their voices made a song in the evening air. They treasured their rare time alone, and Anna May knew they'd be in a good mood when they came back in the house.

"Mom, Pop, I want to talk to you about something," she began when her parents returned and settled in their chairs.

They looked at her silently and waited.

"I've been writing to this lady; her name is Mrs. Entwhistle...."

"Writing to her?" Mom asked, her eyebrows twin question marks. "Who is she, and why would you do that?"

Anna May stumbled through the explanation of why and how she'd gotten in touch with a stranger. Mom's face darkened when she mentioned the connection to Jonas Hershberger.

"We don't talk about him," she said warningly.

"But why don't we?" Anna May said, forgetting to be careful in her urgency to make herself understood. "He left the church long ago. It's ancient history now. And why is it so terrible to think about things in a different way? If we really believe what we say we do, it shouldn't threaten us to hear about other ways."

"Anna May!" Pop's voice was a growl. "Don't talk to your mother like that."

"I don't mean to be disrespectful." Anna May was close to tears. "I'm just asking you to meet Mrs. Entwhistle and her friend, Mrs. Gober, and then make up your mind if I could visit. They'd like to come by tomorrow. I said they could."

She held her breath. Mom and Pop exchanged a look.

"Well, looks like it's settled, then. We wouldn't turn away visitors one of our children invited," Pop said slowly.

"But you should have asked us first," her mother added.

"I know I should have. I guess I'm not going about this very well. Look, I don't want to go on rumspringa and act all crazy; I just want to visit an old lady in a small town. Mrs. Entwhistle said she'd love to have me, if it's all right with you.

She's a good person; you'll see when you meet her."

Pop stood and stretched. "After we meet her, we'll decide."

There was nothing else to say. Silently, Mom blew out the kerosene lanterns one by one. She didn't even say gude nacht.

~*~

Sunday morning was dark and drizzly. The family sat quietly in the living room after the necessary morning chores were done. Even though there was no church service, activity was strictly limited in observance of the Sabbath. Reading was limited to the Bible or devotional books, and Anna May stared at the same page in the book of Acts for a long time. If the weather had been better, she could have at least walked down the lane to the road, but she was trapped in the house by the rain.

Mom was still not talking much and casting dark looks at Anna May. Pop seemed oblivious to the tension in the room. He was actually dozing when the sound of a car making its way down their long lane brought them all to their feet. The little kids rushed to the windows, glad for a distraction on this dismal day. Mom and Pop drew themselves up and stood together in solidarity. Anna May hovered behind them.

Pop opened the door as Mrs. Entwhistle raised her hand to knock.

"Good morning, I'm Cora Entwhistle, and this is my friend, Maxine Gober," Mrs. Entwhistle said, smiling and holding eye contact.

"Yah, we knew you was coming," Pop said, standing aside. "Please come on in."

Mom said nothing, but she did give her visitors a small smile and nod.

Anna May stepped forward. "You are welcome in our home. Can I get you a cup of coffee?" she asked.

"Why, honey, that would just hit the spot," Maxine said, beaming. "What a beautiful farm you have. It's like a picture postcard. As we drove up the lane, we both said at the same time how pretty it is. The white buildings and fences, the bright green of the grass and trees, the golden fields! It must be wonderful to live in such a place. And it's not only natural beauty; anyone can tell how hard you work to keep it just right."

Few people could resist Maxine's warmth, and Mom thawed visibly. "Kom rein," she said, ushering her visitors into the kitchen and indicating seats at the table. She cut a home-made coffee cake into generous slabs and placed the plates and fragrant cups of coffee before her guests.

Mrs. Entwhistle knew good food was one of life's most effective social lubricants, and she was quick to appreciate the effort that had been made.

"Why, Mrs. Bontrager, this is delicious! Do you eat

like this all the time? I'd be as big as that barn out there if I was this good a cook."

Mom tried to hide her pride. "Oh, it's chust a little something the kids like," she said modestly.

Conversation progressed more easily after that. Mrs. Entwhistle described what they'd seen on their tour bus so far. Maxine chimed in with praise for the Seltzberg Inn.

"It was started by an Amish man," Pop said. "Did you know that? Well, he ain't Amish no more, but he used to be when I grew up with him. He was always a real smart kid, and he—"

Pop's voice trailed off when he realized he'd been praising an apostate to two outsiders. He cleared his throat uneasily and glanced at Mom for help. She jumped in, looking directly at Mrs. Entwhistle. This was a dialogue between mothers.

"Anna May said you've been writing to each other."

"Yes, I've so enjoyed her letters. She has beautiful handwriting and expresses herself well," Mrs. Entwhistle said.

"Yah, Anna May was always real smart in school. She's a good girl," Mom said pointedly. "And now she says she wants to visit you. What do you think about that?"

Mrs. Entwhistle paused and took a sip of her coffee to give herself time to think. "I would love to have her visit, but only if it's all right with you."

Mom nodded. "What would she do if she came? She don't sit around at home, she's used to working."

"And I'd work at Mrs. Entwhistle's house," Anna May interjected. "I already told her what all I could do to help her."

"But it wouldn't be all work, would it? There'd be some other activities, like maybe you'd take her to places we wouldn't like for her to go."

"Where would that be?" Mrs. Entwhistle genuinely wanted to know.

"Well, like movies and such. Roller skating. Bowling. I don't know what all," Mom said.

Mrs. Entwhistle grinned. "You sure don't have to worry about roller skating. I don't know what you might find objectionable, but I'm an old lady and there isn't a lot of goings-on at my house. I'm afraid Anna May would be bored rather than contaminated. But you must judge as you see fit. I know you put your daughter's best interests first, always. I do the same for my children."

Mrs. Entwhistle had a feeling she was advocating for a lost cause. She saw Mom gather herself to speak just as the kitchen door banged open, hitting the wall with a crash. They all looked up, startled, to see a young man fall to his knees and crawl across the threshold. Blood ran down his face from a cut on his forehead.

"H'lo, Mom," the young man said, grinning sloppily. "Pop, I wrecked th' car. Again."

With that, he collapsed gently onto the pristine floor. The fumes of alcohol emanating from his body filled the kitchen.

Mrs. Entwhistle and Maxine stared in horror, frozen in their chairs. Pop got to his feet, weariness etched in every line of his body. He grabbed the boy under the arms and hauled him to his feet.

"Come on, Levi. Let's get you cleaned up," he said, half carrying, half dragging the limp body. He shuffled toward the stairway, bowed under the weight of his son's bad decisions.

Mom sat very still, her eyes downcast. When she looked up, her face was grim.

"All right, Anna May," she said, "You can go."

~*~

The tour bus driver wasn't so sure about taking on another passenger in mid-run. "I have to check," he said several times.

"Well, you do that," Mrs. Entwhistle snapped. Her patience was wearing thin. What earthly difference would it make if one more small person sat on the bus? She'd already offered to pay Anna May's fare.

Maxine cast a weather eye at the two spots of pink on Mrs. Entwhistle's cheeks and stepped forward. "Why, honey," she said to the driver, "I don't know that you'd need to bother your boss about this. Anna May's just a little girl, she won't take up hardly any room, and you know we've got empty seats on the bus. I expect the paperwork would be extra work for you, the phone calls, getting permission and all, but is it really necessary? She's of age and her parents gave permission, although she doesn't need it. You know what? If I were you, I'd just tuck Anna May into a seat and not say a word."

"She can't ride free, though," the driver said thoughtfully.

"No, but why don't you just keep her fare for yourself, compensation for your bother. Think of it as a tip for exceptional service from a grateful passenger. Nobody has to know a thing about it."

Mrs. Entwhistle turned her head to stare at Maxine, amazed at her display of chicanery. Her old friend never ceased to surprise her.

The driver chewed the inside of his lower lip for a moment, clearly struggling between caution and greed. Predictably, greed won.

"I oughtn't," he said, "but I will, just as a favor to you two ladies."

Mrs. Entwhistle slipped him some folded bills which disappeared magically into his pocket. She beckoned to Anna May, who'd been waiting a distance away. The girl grabbed her little suitcase and ran to the bus. She made herself small in the seat the bus driver indicated and tried, but failed to keep her eyes down.

The sight of an Amish girl, complete with black

dress, white apron, and white head covering brought the other passengers up short as they entered the bus.

"Hello, what have we here?" It was the appalling Frank. "A new face on the bus! Are you a hitch-hiker, honey?"

"No, sir, I'm going home with Mrs. Entwhistle for a visit."

"What'd you do with your horse and buggy? Who's gonna pick the corn and slop the hogs?" He loomed over her laughing at his own humor, blasting stale coffee breath as Anna May ducked her head shyly.

Mary Alice, his wife gave an exasperated sigh and poked him sharply in the back. "Move it, Frank, people are trying to get by."

Anna May made herself even smaller as the rest of the passengers entered.

Mrs. Entwhistle and Maxine thought the trip home was much more fun when seen through Anna May's eyes. Not once did she say she was tired of sitting or ask when they'd arrive. Her rapt face was turned to the window intent on the passing scenery.

"I've never been this way before, but I almost feel like I'm coming home," she said.

Chapter Five

There's no dance like the happy dance of a dog greeting his returning human. Roger, old as he was, pirouetted and spun like a ballerina when he saw Mrs. Entwhistle. The minute Jackie, the kennel attendant, set him on the floor, he went into fits of joy. Mrs. Entwhistle knelt, arthritic knees crackling, to allow him to cover her face and glasses with kisses.

"Was he a good boy?" she asked apprehensively. "Did he cry? Did he eat? And sleep?"

"He didn't eat the first day, but after that he did fine," Jackie said. "I think he kind of enjoyed keeping track of all the other dogs. No, we didn't allow him in the play yard with them. He only went out alone," she hurried to add. Mrs. Entwhistle's instructions had been abundantly clear about that. "But he liked to touch noses through the fence and do a little barking himself."

Satisfied, Mrs. Entwhistle allowed Jackie to carry all Roger's accoutrements to Maxine's car while she carried Roger.

"Come on, Rog, we're going home," she said into his silky ear. He laid his head on her shoulder, exhausted by his own exuberance.

Anna May was waiting, and Roger sniffed her perfunctorily. Another stranger. He snorted to get her smell out of his nose. All he wanted was his spot at the end of Mrs. Entwhistle's bed.

~*~

Mrs. Entwhistle slept later than usual the next day, and when she awoke it was to the smell of bacon frying. She lay still for a moment trying to puzzle out who was in her kitchen before the events of the last couple of days came back to her.

"Well, it must be Anna May," she said to Roger. "Let's go see."

In the kitchen, they found Anna May presiding over a stove full of breakfast. "I hope you don't mind," she said as Mrs. Entwhistle entered. "Here, sit down and have some coffee."

Mrs. Entwhistle didn't have the heart to say that she always started her day with tea. "This is good practice in not being so set in my ways," she told herself, taking a big swig. It *was* good coffee, and soon it was followed by a plate heaped with two over-easy fried eggs, generous rashers of bacon, buttered toast and fried potatoes. Mrs. Entwhistle tucked in.

After such a sumptuous breakfast, she had to retire to the porch swing and let things settle. Anna May had no such need. She appeared with a bucket smelling strongly of ammonia and a stack of old newspapers.

"Okay if I use these newspapers? I found them stacked in the garage."

"Well, sure, but what are you going to do? You're not washing windows, are you?"

"If you don't mind," Anna May said, and attacked the nearest window. She scrubbed with a wet rag dipped in ammonia water; then she dried with a crumpled sheet of newsprint. The window sparkled.

"Why, honey, you needn't..." Mrs. Entwhistle began, but Anna May would not be diverted.

"At home, we washed all the windows once a week," she said simply. "Usually on Tuesday. Today's Tuesday."

That was only the beginning. Mrs. Entwhistle prided herself on keeping a clean house, but in the days that followed, Anna May scoured it from top to bottom.

"Not that it needs it," she said tactfully. "But I'm used to working."

Finally, when the girl made her way down to the cellar, Mrs. Entwhistle called a firm halt. "Anna

May, you will not clean another inch until we do something fun," she said firmly. "What would you like to do?"

Anna May didn't hesitate. "Go shopping," she said.

Mrs. Entwhistle's heart sank. She hated shopping, and the thought of trailing after a teenage girl was almost more than she could bear. But she looked around her shining rooms and smiled with as much enthusiasm as she could muster.

"Of course. That's just what we'll do."

But first she called Maxine.

"Can you come, too?" she implored. "You know I'm not a good shopper, and I don't want to spoil it for Anna May by being a wet blanket."

"I'll do you one better," Maxine said, "I'll take her, and you stay home."

"Oh, I couldn't let you do that," Mrs. Entwhistle said hopefully,

Maxine just laughed. "Tell her I'll pick her up in an hour."

~*~

When the shoppers returned, they were laden with bags.

"We went to Wal-Mart!" Anna May said, her eyes glowing. "Well, first to the mall, but I didn't have enough money for anything at those stores. Then we went to Wal-Mart, and then to the Salvation Army. And look what I got!"

She began pulling garments out of bags. Mrs. Entwhistle saw jeans and tee shirts, sneakers and socks, leggings and a tiny little skirt.

"You wouldn't believe how cheap these were," Anna May said with satisfaction. "I don't have much money, just what I could save from my allowance, but I had enough for all this."

"But...Is it okay for you to wear these clothes?" Mrs. Entwhistle asked.

"It's okay while I'm here with you," Anna May said. "I want to dress like everyone else so people don't stare at me."

"Wouldn't your folks be upset?"

"They'd be glad I wasn't doing anything worse. And besides, they won't see me."

Mrs. Entwhistle had her doubts, but reminded herself that Anna May was eighteen, old enough to make her own decisions. She watched as the girl scampered off to try on her new clothes in front of the full-length mirror on the closet door.

Maxine sat down with a plop, shaking her head. "You should have seen the looks she got in her black dress and bonnet. I can't say I blame her for wanting to blend in. It won't hurt her to experiment a little bit. Remember when our girls were into that Goth stuff?"

Mrs. Entwhistle shuddered at the memory. Rusty black clothing that bled in the wash. Hobnail boots, purple lipstick, black nail polish. Somehow she'd held the line against tattoos and threatened Diane with death and dismemberment if she got a piercing. She and Floyd had whispered long into the night about what their daughter was becoming and what they could do to stop it. Answer: nothing. Then, suddenly, it was over. Diane went back to normal clothes; in fact, she got downright frilly.

"I must remember that. All things come to pass; nothing comes to stay," she said.

The change in Anna May was more than clothes-deep. As if by magic, the dutiful Amish girl was replaced by a modern teenager. She still weeded the garden without being asked and continued to keep the house shining, but clearly, she was ready for adventure. Mrs. Entwhistle had no idea what to do with her, but she knew someone who would.

Delilah was still in the honeymoon phase of her new marriage. She didn't even try to hide her starry eyes. Since marrying the town's newest doctor, Sanjay Patel, and flying through the course-work for her pre-law degree, she understandably felt like she had the world on a string. Her little boy from a previous relationship, JJ, was three now, and he greeted Mrs. Entwhistle boisterously when she rang the bell.

"Come see my trunks," he shouted.

Mrs. Entwhistle looked at Delilah quizzically.

"Trucks," Delilah interpreted. "We went to the dollar store."

Mrs. Entwhistle duly admired the row of trucks parading down the center of the dining room table. She remembered when that table had been the pristine pride of Jolly Jensen, the former owner of Delilah's house and much of its furnishings. The table had gleamed under Jolly's care. Now it looked a little beat-up, with smudgy handprints and scuff marks from tiny tires. Mrs. Entwhistle thought it looked happier.

"So, what am I going to do with Anna May?" she asked Delilah as they sipped cups of tea. "Of course, she wants to get out and about, but I have no idea what a young person would like to do."

"Send her to me," Delilah said. "I've got a whole list of errands, and she can come along. We'll have lunch and maybe go to a matinee."

"A movie? I don't know if she'd be allowed..." Mrs. Entwhistle began, but Delilah waved away her objections.

"Don't you worry about it. Just bring her."

Mrs. Entwhistle did, breathing a sigh of relief as she went back to her quiet, empty house for a few hours of respite. She needed time to think, because Maxine had presented her with a startling new idea. It was, as Floyd would have put it, enough to make a fish stare, and Mrs. Entwhistle hadn't seen it coming.

"I've been thinking," Maxine had begun. "My big

old house is getting to be too much for me. Seems like all I do is clean and fix and work in the yard and worry about things, and still I feel like I'm never caught up."

Mrs. Entwhistle could relate. It was a lament frequently heard at their kitchen tables.

"So I've been thinking," Maxine continued, "and I really want your honest opinion on this, Cora: I've been thinking that maybe I'd like to move into one of Shyam's tiny houses."

Shyam and Anjali Patel were the former proprietors of the Patel Paradise Motel. They'd come to the rescue when Mrs. Entwhistle and Maxine met with misadventures on Route 66. Mrs. Entwhistle had been delighted when they showed up in her driveway unexpectedly, announcing that they'd retired, sold the motel and embarked on a tour of the United States in their new motor home.

It was meant to be a short visit, but then Shyam suffered a stroke. During his lengthy recovery, the Patels' son, Dr. Sanjay Patel, met and married Delilah and opened a medical practice in town. The whole family became permanent residents.

After Shyam's recovery, the Patels joined forces with Booger, Mrs. Entwhistle's dubious childhood friend, and started a community of tiny houses on the edge of Booger's farm. That the elegant Indian couple could work in harmony with a guy named Booger had been the most surprising thing Mrs. Entwhistle could think of until now.

She stared at her friend in disbelief and admiration. Maxine sure knew how to slap a trump card down on the table.

"Well, I can see the attraction of a tiny house," Mrs. Entwhistle said thoughtfully, when she'd recovered a bit. She wasn't ready, herself, to downsize, but she had to admit it was certainly a reasonable thing to do.

"Would you come with me to talk to the Patels about it?" Max asked.

"Of course I will. Just say when. What do you think you'll do with your house?"

"That's the thing," Maxine said hesitantly. She looked both shy and excited.

"Out with it," Mrs. Entwhistle said. "You've got something more up your sleeve."

"I was thinking of making my old house into a bed and breakfast." Maxine said in a rush. She sat back and waited for her friend's reaction.

"Swanee! You mean an inn?" Mrs. Entwhistle was flummoxed. "How would you go about it? Do you really want to run an inn?"

"I haven't thought it all through yet. There are zoning codes or ordinances or something that would have to be addressed. Then once I got approval, I'd have to get it ready, probably add bathrooms and redo the bedrooms. I'd need someone to live there and manage things, because I don't want to be a full-time innkeeper, but I'd do the breakfasts. That would be fun, don't you think? I could make my cinnamon rolls a specialty of the house, along with fresh-squeezed orange juice, baked oatmeal, sausages, hash-browns, bacon and eggs."

Mrs. Entwhistle's stomach gave an appreciative growl. She wasn't hungry, but she drooled like Pavlov's dog at the thought of Maxine's cinnamon rolls.

"Well, my land, Max, you're a deep one. You've been thinking about this for a while, haven't you?"

"I have. I didn't want to say anything until I'd talked to Geraldine."

Maxine's daughter lived in Australia but kept in touch with weekly phone calls. Naturally, she'd have to be consulted.

"What did Geraldine say?"

"At first, she didn't think it was a good idea. She was afraid it would be too much for me. But then, after she'd slept on it, she started coming up with ideas and got excited about it. I suggested she come home and run it for me, but she's got that boyfriend down there, you know."

Mrs. Entwhistle knew. They'd had many discussions about the young man from Down Under who had stolen Geraldine's heart, and with it, any chance of her returning to her home town.

"Well, what do you think? Is it doable?" Maxine

looked trustingly at her oldest friend.

Mrs. Entwhistle gave the question serious consideration. "Anything is doable if you put enough work and money into it. I guess the big question is, do you want to sink your retirement savings into what is bound to be a risky venture, and do you want to be tied down to making breakfast for strangers every summer morning?"

Maxine tried to look solemn, but her eyes were sparkling. "I think it would be so much fun! You know how I love to bake. Even if I didn't have guests staying, I could maybe have a little breakfast café. I wouldn't compete with the Busy Bee Diner, I'd aim for ladies who brunch, you know, showers or birthdays, make it special and fancy. It would give me an outlet, something to do to keep me busy."

Mrs. Entwhistle considered that statement. "Are you bored, Max? You never said."

"Not bored, exactly, but I know everyone and everything in this town backwards and forwards. This would be something entirely new to me and to the town. All we have is that one B&B, and it's awful."

It was, indeed, awful. A creaky old house run by a creaky old couple who had gotten progressively more crotchety as they aged. Infrequent guests might be treated to a harangue about what the world was coming to with their bowls of stale cornflakes in the morning, and gripes about the incompetence of government with their watery evening cocoa. Then they'd retire to lumpy beds, threadbare sheets and cobwebby ceilings.

It reminded Mrs. Entwhistle of a song she learned as a child, and she immediately sang it, with Maxine chiming in on harmony.

"In the boarding house where I lived, everything was growing old.

Long gray hairs were in the butter, and the bread had turned to mold.

When the dog died, we had sausage; when the cat died, catnip tea.

When the landlord died, I left there. Spare ribs were too much for me."

"Toooo much for meeeee," Maxine warbled.

They laughed, delighted with themselves and a friendship so long and strong it could transport them back to their grade school days and then redeposit them in the present with hardly a bump. Then they got down to business.

"There's definitely a market for a better B&B, but, Max, are you the one to provide it?"

Maxine ignored the question. "The good thing about it is I'd still have my house if it turned out I didn't like living in a tiny house. I could always move back into it if I wanted to."

"Yes, it would be comforting to know you had that safety net and didn't have to say goodbye to the dear old place."

Maxine had lived in her house almost as long as Mrs. Entwhistle had lived in hers. They loved their old homes, despite the arduous work of keeping them up.

"What about money?" Mrs. Entwhistle asked diffidently.

Money and sex were two things they didn't discuss, but she felt she had to break that unspoken rule now.

"I want to talk to Mr. Dansinger, but I think I have enough."

Mr. Dansinger was their mutual banker. Mrs. Entwhistle liked to say he was as patient as Job and as smart as Steve Jobs. Over the years, they'd called on his excellent brain to help them figure out everything from ransom demands to the disposal of a priceless ruby. Mrs. Entwhistle knew the sight of her and Maxine gave Mr. Dansinger a shiver of apprehension, but a thrill of excitement, too.

"I've got an appointment to see him this afternoon," Maxine continued "I hope you can go with me."

"Yes, I'm free. Anna May is spending the day with Delilah. I wouldn't miss a chance to watch Mr. Dansinger's eyes light up when he sees us coming."

Chapter Six

"I've never been to a movie before," Anna May confessed to Delilah. "I can't believe the things they got away with saying. And showing. The language! And the clothes. I loved the clothes."

They'd seen a G-rated Disney film, so tame that Delilah could have felt comfortable taking JJ to see it. But it represented greater freedom than any Anna May had ever known.

Anna May was wearing jeans and a crop top. Her pale hair was unbraided and rippled almost to her waist. Delilah noticed the appreciative glances Anna May got from the teenage theater employees. The contrast of her appearance and her obvious innocence made for a volatile mix.

"It's a big world, Anna May," Delilah said. "The more you explore it, the more you'll feel at home in it. You have a lot of catching up to do. The county fair starts tonight. Would you like to go?"

"Oh, I'd love to! Pop took us to the county fair once, but it was during the day. We just went to the livestock shed to see the 4-H winners. Levi and I begged to go on one ride, but Pop said no."

"Let me check with Sanjay. We'd talked about taking JJ, but hadn't made firm plans yet. I'll call him at the office."

Sanjay was game "It's something I've never done," he confessed, just like Anna May. "I was always studying."

Sanjay had been at or near the top of every class he'd ever taken right through medical school, but he'd always had to work hard for his good grades. Now that he was through with school and established in family practice, he intended to relax a bit and have some of the fun he'd missed.

So the Patels packed up the car and set off an evening of cotton candy and carnival rides. Anna May pulled her hair up in a pony tail, looking like a typical teenager. No way would anyone guess she was Amish. She and JJ shared the back seat.

"Ammay, Ammay!" JJ's voice squeaked with excitement. "We go fair!"

"What *is* a fair?" Anna May asked him teasingly.

The little boy cocked his head to one side. "It's *fair*, Ammay!" he said. "We go fair."

"Okay, JJ, we go fair."

He clutched her hand tightly as he asked that eternal question of childhood: "Are we there yet?"

The midway was crowded with children high on sugar and anticipation. JJ looked on in wonder as those children screamed and ran, wielding their candied apples like swords. It took only a few minutes before he joined them. Sanjay and Delilah were happy to let Anna May keep up with him, which she did, grabbing his chubby hand when he got too far away.

When they came to a ball-toss booth, JJ stopped, transfixed by the giant black and white panda regally presiding on a high shelf.

"I want," he breathed, pointing.

"Oh, JJ, that bear is a prize for people who are really good at throwing the ball," Anna May said.

"You throw ball."

The young man behind the counter grinned at them. "Yeah, c'mon, honey, take a chance for your little kid."

"He's not mine," Anna May said, blushing. "I'm just...a friend. I couldn't hit any of those targets."

"Aw, come on, darlin'. Give it a try. Only a quarter. Just hit three of them little duckies and you win a prize."

"Ammay, you throw ball," JJ said forcefully, gazing straight into her eyes. "You can do it."

The boy behind the counter winked and held out

a ball. Anna May sighed and fished a quarter out of her pocket. Her first throw went wild, but she hit the targets with the next two.

"Try again, sweetheart. Just another quarter," the boy said.

Anna May thought he was cute with his jet-black hair and melting brown eyes. She smiled at him.

"Aw, look at them dimples!" he said. "I bet you'll win this time. Hang on a minute."

He went behind the plywood backdrop and returned with a bucket of different colored balls. "Here, use these."

Anna May hefted one in her hand. It felt different, more like the ones she used to play softball with her brothers and sisters. She aimed and tossed; a duckie bit the dust. JJ hopped up and down with excitement. When she threw a second time, she hit another target. Taking a deep breath, she let loose her third throw. JJ's shout of triumph rang out.

"You dood it, Ammay, you hitted it. I get panda!"

The boy behind the counter locked eyes with Anna May. "The bear is the prize if you do that six times in a row," he said, "but I'll tell you what I'm gonna do. I'm gonna break the rules and let you have that bear." He pulled down the giant panda from the shelf and came around the counter. "Here you go, buddy."

The bear was almost as big as JJ. When he

clutched it tightly around its middle, they looked like they were dancing. But Anna May's attention was on the boy, who stood a little too close.

"Hey, I'm Joey," he said. "What's your name?"

"Anna May."

"That's a pretty name. Well, Anna May, what say we get to know each other better? I'm off work at eleven; meet me then?"

"Oh, no, I can't, I'm, uh, I came with friends, and they won't stay that long. JJ has to get to bed."

"The fair's in town for a week. I work every night, but maybe I could come and see you during the day. We could meet somewhere."

"I don't think so," Anna May said, but her eyes said something else.

"Tell me where you live. I'll come get you. I got a motorcycle and I'll take you for a ride you won't forget."

~*~

Errol Dansinger listened to Maxine's ideas with his fingers steepled. His eyes never left her face as she talked. Mrs. Entwhistle could almost hear the gears meshing in his excellent brain. When Max finished and fell silent, he thought a minute, then spoke.

"Most people your age prefer to reduce the tension and stress in their lives. Yet you're thinking of taking on a project that would challenge those many years your junior. Are you sure this is what you want?"

"Well, not one hundred per cent," Maxine admitted. "I'm pretty sure I want to try tiny house living, and I thought this would be a good way to hang onto my house in case I want to come back to it. I like to entertain, and I love to cook, so it just seems like an opportunity for me to do both."

"In that case, give me a day or two to review your finances. Your late husband made some very wise investments that have appreciated handsomely. You haven't touched the capital since he passed, except to replace your car."

"I really haven't paid much attention to my investments, I'm afraid," Maxine said. "Just let me know what you think I could risk without putting myself in the poor house. I'll talk to some contractors and get an idea of the cost to make my house into a B&B. And I'll talk to Shyam and Anjali Patel about what a tiny house would cost."

"Let's meet again next week and compare notes when we have more information," Mr. Dansinger said, standing to escort the ladies to the door with his usual courtliness. "It's been a pleasure to see you both, as always."

On the sidewalk, they exchanged a conspiratorial grin. "Busy Bee?" Mrs. Entwhistle asked. "The donut sign is on."

"By all means," Maxine replied, leading the way. "I need sugar!"

The Busy Bee Diner was the town's watering hole. Mrs. Entwhistle and Maxine were there several times a week and counted it a good day if they arrived when the Fresh Donuts sign was lighted. They found a table and waved to Carol Ann.

"The usual?" she called.

The ladies nodded. When their donuts arrived, they fell on them with unladylike gusto.

"There's nothing like money talk to make a person hungry," Maxine observed.

Finished, they pushed away the empty plates and patted their lips with brown paper napkins. Carol Ann dropped their bill on the table as she rushed by.

"Tell Harvey we enjoyed 'em," Mrs. Entwhistle said.

She saw Herve' grimace behind the counter when he heard his name mangled. Again. The poor man had long ago become Harvey to most of the town, but she knew he'd never reconciled himself to the loss of his proud Mexican name.

"I mean, Herve'," she corrected herself, fluttering her fingers at him. But it was too late. He turned away pointedly to demonstrate his hurt feelings.

"Now let me see," Maxine said. She reached for her purse, rummaged through it until she found her phone and pulled up the tip calculator app. Squinting, she entered the amount of the bill with one finger. "Do you think a fifteen or twenty percent tip?"

"Well, Carol Ann brought us our donuts right away while they were still hot, so let's do twenty percent today. I think she has to split her tips with Harvey, and he did a good job, too. Plus, I hurt his feelings. Yes, twenty percent."

"Okay." Maxine poked in some more numbers, but shook her head at the result. "That doesn't look right."

"All we have to do is take ten percent of the total, double it and that's our twenty percent tip. Wait, I've got my calculator right here," Mrs. Entwhistle said. "I'll add it up."

It took a while, but finally they felt satisfied with the math.

"Shall we just split the bill in half?" Mrs. Entwhistle asked.

"No, honey, I had the éclair and you only had a glazed, so mine was a little more."

"Yes, but I got an extra donut to take home, so figure that in my part."

"And I got a glass of orange juice."

The calculator was put to work again. Maxine got out her little notebook and pen to keep track of the totals. At last, they reached the exact amount they each owed.

Mrs. Entwhistle dug through her billfold. "Darn it, I don't have anything but a twenty and three ones. Let me put it all on my charge card, and you can pay me."

"I don't have the right change, either," Maxine said. "But I can give you this ten, and then you can pay me back $5.53 when you break your twenty."

"Oh, I'm afraid I'll forget. Here, let me check my change. Maybe I have enough." She dumped the contents of her change purse on the table and began counting.

At the next table, two men who'd enjoyed a similar repast pushed back their chairs. One of them reached in his pocket, extracted a couple of crumpled bills and tossed them on the table. "I got it," he said. His companion nodded. They left.

Mrs. Entwhistle and Maxine, still deep in calculations, didn't even look up. Maxine was digging through her purse again.

"Wait a minute," she said. "I think I have a gift certificate."

They started over.

Chapter Seven

After Mrs. Entwhistle and Maxine left the Busy Bee Diner, they went to Maxine's house. They looked at the familiar old structure with new eyes—bed and breakfast eyes.

"There are four bedrooms upstairs, but only one bathroom. I think I'd need each bedroom to have its own bath, don't you think?" Maxine said.

"Yes, I'd say so, to get the best kind of guests. People don't want to share bathrooms these days. And you'd want to get top dollar if you're going to all that trouble. I mean, c'mon, you're going to bake your cinnamon rolls!"

They climbed the wide oak staircase to the second floor. A long central hallway ran down the middle, ending in an arched, stained-glass window. The light was reflected in a dazzle of jewel-like prisms. Solid wooden doors with crystal knobs led to four large, square bedrooms and one old-fashioned bath. Maxine opened the nearest door.

"It's a big room," Mrs. Entwhistle observed, trying to see it as if she hadn't been familiar with that space for more than half a century. "Pretty little fireplace. But the closet is small, and the bathroom's down the hall."

"From what I've read about B&Bs, you don't need big closets. Guests don't bring their whole wardrobes; they just need a small space and a few nice hangers. But where would I add a bathroom?"

"It's a big room—they all are—but you'll have to hire someone to plan it for you," Mrs. Entwhistle said firmly. "We don't have the right skill set to do that."

"I think the furniture is okay, though," Maxine said, throwing open each door on the hall.

Old-fashioned four-poster beds, polished maple chests and rag rugs over gleaming hardwood floors looked back at them. Maxine liked a uniform look from the street, so each window was draped with plain white cotton curtains, starched and ironed to perfection. The beds all wore counterpanes of dazzling whiteness. The effect was simple and immaculate.

"I can't see a thing you need to change. You might want to add some pillows and throws for color and put up a few more pictures, but the rooms look very inviting to me. You could advertise them as having old-time comfort with modern conveniences."

"Which I don't have."

"Yet. What about the main bedroom and bathroom downstairs?" Mrs. Entwhistle asked.

"That will be the manager's suite," Maxine said. "I'll need someone on site to take care of things."

"But who?"

"No idea. But surely someone in town will be looking for a job."

The Rolodex in Mrs. Entwhistle's head spun rapidly but came up empty. "I can't think of anyone. The people I know best are mostly living in the Shady Rest Assisted Living Center now. They're past the time in their lives when they'd want to take on something like this."

"I'll ask around when the time comes. Our friends have sons and daughters and grandchildren. There'll be someone."

Maxine led the way downstairs, where they surveyed what would be the public rooms. *How odd to think of Maxine's house having public rooms!*

"I'd leave the dining room pretty much as it is," Maxine said, standing in the doorway.

The large table easily accommodated ten with the leaf in. A sideboard could be a serving buffet. Maxine loved to set a pretty table and had drawers full of tablecloths, placemats and napkins. Mrs. Entwhistle knew breakfast in this house would be a special occasion with linen placemats and fresh flowers.

They went into the kitchen.

"Lucky I had this redone a couple years ago," Maxine said with satisfaction. "Nothing to do in here but cook. But what about the sitting room?"

It was a well-proportioned room at the front of the house. In the morning, light streamed in through the long windows, illuminating the comfortable furniture. A brick fireplace burned wood, although Maxine seldom bothered to light it anymore. The hassle of hauling in wood and cleaning out ashes was just too much. But both ladies envisioned a cozy fire and guests gathered around with glasses of wine or cups of hot chocolate. They nodded at each other.

"Don't change a thing," Mrs. Entwhistle said. "But what about outside? People like to eat outside in the summer."

"Hmm, I hadn't thought that far. I guess—the patio?"

Maxine's patio had definitely seen better days. As much as she herself liked to dine al fresco, it was inexplicable that she'd neglected the space, but she had. Weeds struggled to grow up through the cracks in the concrete and the wrought-iron table and chairs needed a good wire-brushing and painting. The umbrella over the table tilted at a crazy angle, and the one decorative planter held a forlorn geranium.

"Oh." Maxine said in a small voice.

"Nothing that can't be remedied." Mrs. Entwhistle pulled out one of the rusty chairs and sat down. "Now. Let's think about resources and money."

~*~

Anna May was quiet on the way home from the fair. JJ snuggled into his car seat and slept immediately, done in by excitement. Even in sleep, he clutched the paw of the giant bear that rode beside him. Anna May gazed out the window at the gathering dusk.

"How is your visit going?" Sanjay asked over his shoulder from the front seat. "Is it what you expected? Are you enjoying yourself?"

"Yah, I'm having a wonderful time. I miss the family, especially the little ones, but I needed this. At home, everything is always the same. You know?" Anna May's voice was wistful.

Delilah heard and understood. Teenage years could be a time when real life seemed so far away as to be forever unattainable. Longing for new, grown-up experiences could become an itch that was dangerous to scratch. She ought to know. She glanced ruefully at her son, the product of an ill-fated affair with her high school teacher. She couldn't possibly have loved her little boy more, but she did wish his start in life had been more conventional. Now that she was a settled, married woman, she felt she'd looked at life from both sides, as the song said.

"But isn't it a little quiet, living with an older lady?" Delilah asked. "I mean, I love Mrs. Entwhistle to death, but she isn't going out dancing every night. Or any night. Are you bored? You didn't come all this way to pull weeds and make crock-pot suppers. What do you want to get out of your visit?"

Anna May thought for a moment. "We Amish have something called rumspringa. Young people can go 'high,' that's what we call it, for a while. They leave home, stay in apartments with other kids, and drive cars—live like they think the English do. Only some of the kids get into drinking and drugs. Seems a lot of them have car wrecks. We aren't used to driving anything but horses, you know. My brother, Levi, is going wild on rumspringa. He still lives at home and works on the farm during the day, but he has a car and at night he goes out. He's come home in pretty bad shape, and my folks have to deal with it."

"And that's okay with them?" Delilah's eyes were wide.

"Not okay, exactly, but accepted for now. They hope he'll get all the wildness out of his system and be ready to join the church, get married to a nice Amish girl and have a family. My teacher called rumspringa a rite of passage."

"But you didn't want to do all that," Sanjay said.

"No. Watching Levi, it looked more like torture than fun. But I did want to get away from the farm and experience new things. I didn't think Mom would let me go even after Mrs. Entwhistle and Maxine came to the house to meet them. But then Lee stumbled into the kitchen, drunk as a skunk, and next thing you know, Mom said I could come." Anna May shook her head, still surprised. "I guess she thought a tame visit with an old lady couldn't be so bad."

Delilah's laugh rang out. "She didn't know *this* old lady. Mrs. Entwhistle may seem to lead a quiet life, but just wait. Tame is the last word I'd use."

Chapter Eight

Levi hated himself. Rumspringa was getting old. Getting drunk every weekend had lost its appeal. The white powder he sometimes sniffed left him feeling sad and jittery when it wore off. Worst of all was the feeling of disappointing his parents.

"You shoulda moved out," his friend Elmer said. "It ain't no good going home to the parents all jammed up. They don't want to know about it. And then your Pop makes you work all day in the field when you can't hardly stand. You should come live in the apartment with us guys."

Levi had spent a lot of time in that apartment. Located above the town's drugstore, it consisted of three huge rooms without central heat or air. The kitchen was a linoleum-topped counter with a microwave and a cast iron sink. The beer was kept in an iced-down cooler, when anyone could remember to buy ice. Otherwise, they drank it warm. The rooms were brutally cold in the winter and breathlessly hot in the summer. Mattresses were tossed around on the floor, competing with the dust bunnies for space. On any given night, an assortment of Amish kids on rumspringa could be found sleeping, toking, smoking and drinking. Some were throwing up in a bathroom that was too gross for words.

In contrast, there was the serenity of his bedroom at home, where clean sheets smelled of sunshine, and sparkling windows looked over his father's fields. Every morning when he was a kid he'd look out past the big white barn, over the work horses switching their tails against flies, beyond the cows plodding single-mindedly out to pasture, to the fields golden with wheat and green with corn. He'd always thought of the Bible verse: "This is the day that the Lord has made; rejoice and be glad in it." He wouldn't have admitted that to anyone now.

I'm a drunk. I got an eighth-grade education and can't find a job because I don't know nothin' but farming. My car's in the junkyard. I feel like crap all the time. This ain't no way to live.

~*~

Seven hundred miles away, Levi's sister greeted her day. Anna May's eyes opened in Diane Entwhistle's old bedroom, still wallpapered in big cabbage roses, still filled with posters of movie stars who had become middle-aged men. She lay still for a moment, thinking of her hostess. Mrs. Entwhistle had apologized for the accommodations.

"I haven't changed a thing since Diane got married," she said. "And I just have one bathroom that we'll have to share."

Anna May laughed. "There are a whole lot more of us at home sharing one bathroom. I don't mind, but I'm sorry if I get in your way."

"Nonsense, child. I came up in a tougher time. No thoughts of private baths then. Indoor plumbing was as good as it got."

"We still have an outhouse for emergencies," Anna May confessed. "The spiders love it. Nobody lingers, I can tell you that."

"Oh, I remember those days well," Mrs. Entwhistle said, smiling. "Grandpa kept his outhouse even after he had a septic tank dug. Just in case, he said."

"Speaking of Grandpa, I sure would like to see his farm," Anna May said.

"That's what we'll do today," Mrs. Entwhistle said. "I haven't been out to the old place for a donkey's age. I'd like to see it, too."

"What about the people who live there? Won't they mind?" Anna May asked.

"They're distant cousins of yours. They'll be delighted."

Louise and Henry Hersherger and their children were in the farmyard when Mrs. Entwhistle puttered up in her scooter with Anna May rosy and giggling in the sidecar. Good mornings were exchanged, and Mrs. Entwhistle introduced her guest.

"This is Anna May Bontrager. Her mother was a Hershberger, and Jonas Hershberger was Anna May's ancestor."

"He was Mom's great-grandpop," Anna May said.

"Oh, that would make us, let's see, third cousins once removed?" Louise said.

"I never could get those relationships straight in my head," Mrs. Entwhistle observed.

"But we're distantly related somehow," Henry said, "and you are very welcome. This is where our ancestor, Jonas, raised his family. Let us show you around."

Henry and Louise ushered Mrs. Entwhistle and Anna May around the grounds while free-range chickens pecked at their feet. The children captured Anna May's hand and tugged her to the hayloft to see the latest batch of kittens. She came down with straw in her hair and a look of total contentment on her face.

"I felt right at home there," she said to Mrs. Entwhistle later. "It's like I could feel great-great-grandfather's spirit or something, and he was saying 'Wilkum.' Do you believe in things like that?"

Mrs. Entwhistle pursed her lips. "I can't say that I do, honey, but if I'm honest, I must tell you that I have been to a fortune-teller before. Twice."

Anna May's eyes widened. "Oh, tell me about it!"

Mrs. Entwhistle and Maxine had on two occasions consulted with a certain Madame Esmeralda, the first time at the county fair when she advised Mrs. Entwhistle not to buy the car she was planning on buying.

"I didn't buy it, but not because she said so," Mrs. Entwhistle said.

Maxine had dragged her back to the seer once again when she was puzzled and upset about a valuable gem she'd found among Floyd's belongings after his death.

"Esmeralda said some stuff about it, nothing very helpful, and then she told me never to come back," Mrs. Entwhistle said.

"Why?"

"She admitted she didn't really have visions except with me, and she didn't like the feeling it gave her. Somehow, that was my fault, I guess. Anyway, I never went back and don't plan to. Do Amish believe in the supernatural?"

"I don't think they'd label it like that, but many of our people are superstitious. Maybe a better word would be gullible. I think it's because, as a group, we aren't very educated, so we're apt to believe in something like a faith healer. Mom goes to the foot doctor, and she thinks it helps her arthritis."

"What's a foot doctor?"

"I don't know about all of them, but the one in our community presses on your feet and he says that affects different spots in the body. Like if you had a toothache, he'd press one place, or if you had a sore back, another place."

"Hmmm. Reflexology, I think it's called. Did this foot doctor get any training? Does he have a license of some kind?"

"No. He read some books, I guess, or maybe another foot doctor showed him. A lot of Amish go to him first before they go to a medical doctor. For one thing, we can get to his place in a buggy. When we go to a regular doctor, we have to hire someone to drive us there."

"Hire someone? Like an Uber?"

"We just ask a neighbor. Our English neighbors are real good about taking us when we need to go. It's a hassle, though, making all the arrangements. Without telephones, we can't just call them up; we have to go to their house to ask. And it can be expensive. We always pay the driver for gas and mileage."

"Forgive me, Anna May, if I'm asking an impertinent question," Mrs. Entwhistle said. "I get that Amish think owning a car is wrong and they use a horse and buggy instead. But isn't it also wrong to pay to ride in someone else's car?"

"I don't know how to answer that. It's just something we do." Anna May looked troubled. "We do it when we have to, like when there's a baby coming, or somebody's sick or in an accident. Maybe it *is* wrong."

"Child, don't mind me. Sometimes my curiosity gets the best of me, and I forget my manners. If your family and church say car rides are okay in some circumstances, who am I to question it? I'm just that goofy octogenarian who rides a pink Vespa!"

They both laughed and the subject was dismissed, but Anna May thought about it that night in her bed.

Amish people drew a line at a certain point in history, and agreed not to cross it. Why? Who decided that some modern inventions were bad, and keeping to ourselves was good? Why is it important to stay "off the grid?" Are English folks who use electricity to cool their refrigerators somehow morally worse people than Amish who have a generator to do the same job?

Anna May didn't know the answers to her own questions. She felt disloyal for even asking them. Sleep was elusive that night.

~*~

Maxine couldn't decide, and there were a lot of decisions to be made. Should she open the inn "as is," or do a major remodel? Should she try to run it herself at first, just to get the feel of it, or start with an on-site manager? What about her new home? There were three occupied homes in the tiny house village and one under construction. She could buy the one being built and pick the finishes. It couldn't have worked out better. But something was stopping her from pulling the trigger. She wasn't sure what.

"I almost wish I'd never started this," she confessed to Mrs. Entwhistle.

"You really haven't started anything yet; you just have an idea. You needn't go through with it if you decide you don't want to."

"I do want to. I think. It's just...."

"Change," Mrs. Entwhistle said, nodding.

"Yes. Change. I don't seem to handle it so well anymore." Maxine sighed ruefully. "I used to pride myself on my resilience, but now change seems overwhelming."

"I know what you mean," Mrs. Entwhistle said. "I feel the same way. Part of me wants to just sit on the porch and rock, but another part of me isn't done living yet. Use it or lose it."

"Or we'll rust like the Tin Woodman," Maxine said. "I know, I know. It's not the work I'm afraid of, it's the unknown. What am I trading my comfortable life for? Maybe I'm too old to make such a drastic change. I don't want to make a misery of my last years on this earth."

"I think you need a list," Mrs. Entwhistle

suggested.

Mrs. Entwhistle and Maxine both loved lists. They believed every daunting prospect could be broken down into steps on a list, and, once committed to paper, could and would be conquered.

"Once you've got a plan it will all fall into place," Mrs. Entwhistle said, getting out a lined yellow pad and a ballpoint pen. "Now: number one. Housing. Where do you want to live?"

"Where *do* I want to live?" Maxine mused. "I thought I wanted a tiny house, but now I'm having doubts. I think it's the lack of storage that has me hung up. What do I do with all my stuff? I've got beautiful crystal and china that mean a lot to me. There won't be a place to put it in a tiny house. Should I try to sell my treasures or give them away or what?"

"Nobody wants them," Mrs. Entwhistle said bluntly. "You can ask your daughter, but I'd lay money on a turn-down. Young people these days don't clutter up their lives with stuff that can't go into the dishwasher."

"I could rent a storage unit," Maxine said.

"And pay for storing things you never use and nobody else wants? And then when you're gone, Geraldine will have to come back from Australia and figure out what to do with all of it?"

"Well, when you put it that way. But what, then?"

"Most of it was wedding presents, right?"

"Right."

"So, you've had it for fifty-plus years. Do you still love it?"

"Yes."

"Then use it yourself."

"But the crystal is as fragile as soap-bubbles, and the china is Spode. There's a set of sterling silver flatware, too."

"So?"

"What if I break something, or put a silver fork down the garbage disposal?"

Mrs. Entwhistle smiled and shrugged. Maxine looked aghast.

"You've saved this stuff all your life," Mrs. Entwhistle said, "only taking it out maybe once or twice a year on special occasions when it had to be polished and pampered. Now nobody else wants to take on the task, so you might as well enjoy it yourself. Donate your everyday things to the thrift shop, unpack the precious items and put them in your new cabinets. Drink your orange juice from a crystal goblet and eat your scrambled eggs with a sterling fork off a Spode plate."

Maxine thought for a moment, then a small smile tugged at her lips. "You know, I think I will. It's just stuff, right? I'll use it, and maybe I'll lose it and so what? Figuring out that one problem feels like a relief. Maybe I can figure out the rest."

"I know you can, honey. I've watched you figure things out for years."

Chapter Nine

Mrs. Entwhistle had never in her life done so much listening. Anna May seemed to have sprung a leak in the talking department. She started at breakfast and pretty much talked the whole day. And it wasn't just idle chatter.

"I don't know what to do next," she said over and over, echoing Maxine. "I feel like I can't go back home, but I don't belong here, and I can't impose on you forever."

Here Mrs. Entwhistle murmured hospitable denials, but they were sounding progressively weaker. Much as she loved to be around people, she needed solitude to recharge her batteries. She longed for some peace and quiet in her own home.

"And there's nothing I can do to earn a living," Anna May continued. "I'm not educated or trained to do anything besides weed the garden or plop plates of food in front of people."

"What would your folks say if you didn't go back home?" Mrs. Entwhistle wondered.

"They'd be frantic," Anna May replied promptly. "Having Levi go wild on rumspringa was enough of a burden for them. I can't add to it."

"So then you think you'll go back?" Mrs. Entwhistle tried to keep a hopeful note out of her voice.

"Yah, I should, but I just can't make myself do it."

And then the conversational loop would start all over again. Finally, Anna May would tire of her own indecision and bustle off to do some work. She'd been raised to find solace in labor and she sought it now. Mrs. Entwhistle's perennial borders had never looked so good.

"I don't know what to tell her," she confessed to Maxine when they had a minute to themselves. "The poor girl is obviously miserable, but only she can make the decision, and it's a huge one."

"Would she be shunned if she left the Amish, do you think?" Maxine asked.

"I have no idea. But certainly, she'd be far from her home and family. I think she's young for her age, without much life experience, and she'd be on her own. And she's right when she says she has no viable way of making a living. I guess she could work as a maid or a mother's helper. She's a wonderful housekeeper, can turn her hand to anything, good with people..." She paused and her raised eyebrows perfectly matched Maxine's own.

"Yes," Maxine said thoughtfully, "she knows how to keep a place up to snuff, inside and out."

"And she's bright as a new penny. She could learn to do accounts, order supplies, book reservations, anything."

"Nice personality. Friendly and hospitable by nature."

They were on exactly the same page.

"But her parents might be upset if she were to find a job," Maxine said thoughtfully.

"Anna May is of age. She has to decide for herself."

Anna May straightened up and surveyed the garden. Not a weed dared poke its head above ground. The rows were shining with healthy plants. There would be a bumper crop this year.

She stopped planning future meals in her head and brought herself back to reality. She had overstayed her welcome. Mrs. Entwhistle would never say so, but Anna May knew she had. The thought of returning to her parents' farm, doing barn chores, helping her Mom with the cooking and cleaning, looking after her younger siblings, and trundling to town for her shifts at the restaurant filled her with dismay. There had to be more to life than that.

What if...? What if she could stay on here, in this small Southern town? After all, she sort of had roots here. Maybe she could get a waitress job at the Busy Bee Diner. Or maybe somewhere in town there was a new mother who would welcome some temporary help. She could post a sign on the community bulletin board. But even as these fledgling plans took shape, they died. Not one of those jobs would provide enough money to pay rent and feed and clothe herself.

If only she could continue in school. Anna May knew there were programs for getting a GED, a General Equivalency Diploma. Once she had that, maybe she could find a way to take some college classes. She had no goal in mind except feeding her hunger for knowledge. Somehow, she felt education would light a path to a future she couldn't visualize.

Her mind hurt from churning the same old problems over and over. There had to be a way out. She just couldn't find it.

~*~

Maxine surveyed Anjali Patel's tiny living room doubtfully. "I could never get my furniture in here," she said.

Anjali smiled. "No, my dear, you could not. And you know what that means."

"New furniture?"

"New furniture of a smaller size. What would you like?"

"Well, what I have now is kind of large and dark. It's been in my house for ages. Some of it was my mother's, and some is even older than that. Family antiques. Oh, what would I do with the family antiques?"

"Would your daughter want them?"

"Geraldine lives in Australia. The shipping would be prohibitive."

"Then why not leave them where they are and let the inn visitors enjoy them? But let us put that consideration to one side for now and concentrate on how you would live in a tiny house."

Anjali had developed some good sales techniques since she and Shyam moved into their own miniscule bungalow. The Patels made it look very attractive, and the little community was generating interest. Now Maxine was contemplating joining them, but at the moment, she was awash in doubts.

"Do you like the farmhouse look?" Anjali asked. "White furniture, lots of pillows and throws for color."

"White? Oh, I don't think so. I have Marty. Cat hair, you know."

Marty was Maxine's big yellow tomcat, found abandoned at a stopover on Route 66. He'd already survived his mother being killed, a long stay at the vet's, and an automobile accident, but those experiences had only enhanced his self-confidence. Marty was not only a survivor, but a feisty, alpha one. Roger maintained a respectful attitude in the big cat's presence after having his nose swiped at first acquaintance.

"Slipcovers," Anjali said. "Washable slipcovers, so your furniture is always immaculate. Picture it. Small pieces that fit the space without overwhelming it. Bright accessories that you change with the seasons. Would it not be fun to completely change the look of your house for spring, fall, Christmas?"

"Oh, that would be fun!" Maxine's eyes brightened. "I'd have a blank slate, is that what you mean?"

"Yes, a blank slate. Seasonal pillow covers stashed in your linen closet. Quilts and throws that might stay on your bed except when you want to change the look of your living room."

"But storage? Isn't that a problem?"

"It will surprise you how much of a problem it is *not*, once you have right-sized your possessions," Anjali said. "It is freeing to own only what one wants or needs. Yes, I know it seems impossible when you think of getting rid of so much, but believe me, it can be done."

"I'd still have plenty of room to store things at home," Maxine said thoughtfully. "Things I just couldn't bear to let go. There's the attic and the basement. If it turned out I didn't like tiny house living, I could always go back to my house."

"So what are you worried about?" Anjali's smile was kindness itself. "You have the best of all worlds, dear Max. What is stopping you?"

"I don't trust myself to make the right decisions in a situation that's so new to me. I don't know how to get started with a B&B, how to structure it, who would run it for me; oh, just so many worries and doubts!"

"But Shyam and I know exactly how to do all that. Why have you not asked us?"

"I couldn't impose," Maxine said.

"Nonsense! We love to be busy, and we love you. What could be more natural than helping our dear friend?"

The motorcycle had a distinctive raspy roar, and it sounded close. Mrs. Entwhistle looked out the window and saw a big Harley pulling into her driveway. A black-leather clad young man dismounted and Anna May appeared from where she'd been walking aimlessly in the back yard. Almost as if she were expecting someone. Mrs. Entwhistle watched as the young couple stood close together. The sound of their laughter floated in the air. Anna May flipped her hair back in a way that had nothing to do with being Amish, but everything to do with the apple in the Garden of Eden. Mrs. Entwhistle felt a tickle of foreboding, but Anna May was of age and capable of making her own decisions. She stepped back from the window, determined to mind her own business.

But she couldn't. This girl was a guest in her house, and that put Mrs. Entwhistle in the role of caretaker. Anna May had been sheltered and isolated. She was a baby in terms of worldly experience, perhaps too vulnerable to the charms of this dubious-looking young man. Mrs. Entwhistle opened the door, walked across the lawn and joined them. Anna May turned with a smile.

"Mrs. Entwhistle, this is my friend, Joey. He works at the fair. I met him when I won a big panda bear for JJ."

Mrs. Entwhistle stuck out her hand. She'd found a firm handshake was disconcerting to a certain kind of male, but Joey took her hand, held it and made a sketchy little bow over it.

"Pleased to meet you, ma'am," he said, holding eye contact.

She revised her opinion as she took him in. Poised, self-confident, sure of his charm. A little rough around the edges, to be sure, with a bad boy air about him. Mrs. Entwhistle could see the attraction.

"I'd like to take Anna May for a ride if it's okay with you," Joey said. He was being deferential. "Just around town, maybe out to the old mill. It's a beautiful day, and I don't have to be at work until three. I brought an extra helmet."

"Oh, would it be okay?" Anna May asked. "I'd love to see the old mill. I'm sure it would be safe."

"I ride a scooter myself," Mrs. Entwhistle had to admit, "so I can hardly lecture you on safety. It's up to you, Anna May. You're old enough to decide."

They were up on the motorcycle in a flash. Mrs. Entwhistle watched them put-put sedately down the street, Anna May's arms clutched around Joey's waist. The roar of the bike as Joey tuned it up on the highway reached her ears as a distant warning of things to come.

After that, Joey was a daily presence in Mrs. Entwhistle's house when he called to pick up Anna May around noon. He slept until about then, after working past midnight at the fair. Anna May was always ready and waiting without seeming to be waiting. She wore her hair down now, in a blond cascade. Her eyes were bright and she had a glow about her that didn't come from the make-up she'd started using. In shorts and tight tee-shirts, she'd come a long way from the prim, bonneted Amish girl who'd gotten off the tour bus. Mrs. Entwhistle observed the changes with consternation. If this child got caught up in an unsuitable romance, her parents' worst fears would be realized. She had a feeling she knew who'd be blamed.

Mrs. Entwhistle made an effort to get to know Joey. She felt it was her duty as *in loco parentis*, and besides, in her experience, people were always worth knowing. Even those who seemed the toughest on the outside had a bedrock inner core that told who they really were. She probed gently to find that core in Joey.

"How does your family feel about your working in the carnival business?" she asked, handing him a glass of her special mint iced tea.

"There's just Dad. Mom left when I was two, and we never heard from her after that. I don't know if she's even still alive." Joey's deliverance of such dire information was off-hand. "And Dad's a carnie, too. In fact, he's part-owner of our outfit. Well, he always says he's part-owner of debts and disasters."

"You've been in this business all your life, then?" Mrs. Entwhistle asked.

"Yep. We travel from May through October. The winter months we live in Florida. Dad's got a double-wide close to the beach. It ain't a bad life if you got itchy feet."

"Is Florida where you went to school?"

"Yeah, when I went. I never did graduate from high school. I'd start late every fall and then leave before the school year was up in the spring. That don't make for very good grades. I just say I graduated from the school of hard knocks. That's what my Dad says, too."

"What are your ambitions for the future?" Mrs. Entwhistle hoped he had some.

"Whatever happens, happens," Joey said with a shrug. "It don't work to plan things, not for me. I just take what comes."

"But if you don't have some kind of plan, you'll drift," Mrs. Entwhistle said. "You're in prime time right now. This is when you lay the groundwork for the rest of your life."

Joey shot her a look of such cynicism that she blinked. Just then, Anna May joined them, Joey stood, and they were out the door. Conversation over. But it lingered in Mrs. Entwhistle's mind.

Chapter Ten

Workmen swarmed Maxine's house, ringing the air with the sound of power tools. There was a constant hum of activity, daily crises and triumphs. Orders were delivered or delayed; progress was made or lost; expenses climbed alarmingly, and yet despite all the hubbub, it seemed nothing got finished.

"I don't know how to judge the quality of the work," Maxine confessed to Mrs. Entwhistle. "But I can see the lack of progress and that tools and construction mess are left scattered all over at the end of the day. The men don't seem to have a set schedule; they either show up in the morning, or they don't. I never know what to expect. The general contractor has two other jobs that he's overseeing, and he's dividing his time between them, so he's hard to reach when I have questions."

Anna May was listening. "You need Amish

carpenters," she said.

"Is there such a thing?" Maxine asked.

Anna May laughed. "Just about every Amish man can build anything from a bench to a barn. I wish you could see a barn-raising sometime. When a barn burns down, a crowd of men gathers at dawn to rebuild it. Everyone knows what to do, and they divide up the jobs and get right to work. Seeing them walk the walls up is just amazing. By the end of the day, there's a new barn standing where a big open space used to be. It's such an example of know-how and teamwork. And here's the thing: with Amish workmen, you'd not have to worry that you were getting cheated or that the work was sloppy. They don't work cheap, but they work good."

"But a team of Amish carpenters wouldn't travel this far, would they?"

"Oh, yah, at the right time of the year, they would. Right now, it's not harvest yet, so they could get away for a short time. You'd be surprised how much they could get done in a week."

"But where would they stay?"

"They wouldn't be particular about that. They'd stay four to a room at one of the motels out on the interstate."

Maxine's brain was churning. The prospect of a hard-working, honest crew that she didn't need to watch like a hawk was appealing.

"How would I get in touch with the right person?"

she asked.

"Let me see if I can help with that," Anna May said.

Although there were no telephones in Amish homes, many communities had shared telephones. A shed would be built near the road and connected to the telephone lines. The phone inside was for the use of the Amish families who lived nearby, and they all contributed to the cost. Anna May had never questioned why a home phone was forbidden, but a community phone booth situated in a field was okay. She thought about it now.

She knew, too, that her brother, Levi, had a cell phone, although how he charged it remained a mystery. She tried his number.

"Ammay? Is that you?" Levi sounded out of breath.

"Yah. What are you doing? Sounds like you're running."

"No, just throwing hay bales up in the loft. What's going on?"

"I need to see about getting a carpenter crew to come down here and help my friend, Maxine, with a building project. Do you know anybody who might be interested?"

Anna May went into some detail about Maxine's needs, and Levi listened carefully. "I'd like to come myself," he said. "Let me talk to some of the guys around here and see who's available."

It took a week, but Levi called back and said, "I've got ten men lined up. We rented a van, which I'll drive. We're coming on Saturday. Is your friend ready for us?"

Maxine wasn't, but she got ready in a hurry. First, she fired the contractor and asked him to pack up his gear and his crew and vacate her premises. Next, she drove to the Motel Six and reserved four double rooms.

"But not for Levi," Mrs. Entwhistle said. "He'll stay here with me and Anna May."

Last, she started cooking. Anna May worked beside her, trimming meat, peeling potatoes, showing her how to make dishes she'd never made before in addition to her good Southern cooking.

"They'll expect to eat at least one big meal a day. At harvest time, teams of threshers go from farm to farm, and the wives get together and make huge feasts for the noon meal," Anna May told her.

They cooked on and on, filling Maxine's refrigerator and freezer, then encroaching into Mrs. Entwhistle's. Maxine worried that the food wouldn't be as good as the men were used to at home, but Anna May reassured her. "They'll be so hungry, they won't be picky," she said.

Mrs. Entwhistle marveled at Maxine's calm in the eye of this storm. "Doesn't it drive you crazy, all this commotion and uncertainty?"

"It should, but somehow, it doesn't. I trust Anna May not to steer me wrong. I've got a plan and a trustworthy crew, so now it's just a matter of finally getting it done."

Mrs. Entwhistle shook her head in admiration. "And at the same time, you're working on your tiny house."

"Well, I'm not personally swinging a hammer, but I do have to pick out the finishes and furniture. It's fun. I feel more awake and alive than I have for a long time. Although sometimes, especially when I'm tired, I wonder why I'm going to so much trouble at my age. I mean, all this redecorating and remodeling and building, and I'm eighty years old. How long will I be around to enjoy it?"

"Do you plan to turn up your toes today?"

"Nope."

"Then you've got today. That's all anybody ever has. Might as well make it good."

Mrs. Entwhistle thought one of the most surprising things about being old was the fact that she still felt young inside her head. Oh, sure, her bones creaked and ached sometimes, but life was sweet and full of promise and very much worth living. She knew Maxine felt the same way.

Together they threaded their way through the now empty rooms of Maxine's house. The new *en suite* bathrooms, while still unfinished, were taking shape.

"The bathrooms are small," Maxine said. "To make room for them the closets have become just hang-rods with a shelf above and a luggage rack below."

"I think privacy matters more than size when it comes to bathrooms," Mrs. Entwhistle observed.

"And look at what pretty tile you've chosen. You've got warming rails for the towels and walk-in showers."

"I wanted claw-foot tubs, but there just isn't room."

"Over-rated. Those things are impossible to get in and out of, and forget about cleaning them!"

They went back downstairs to Maxine's bedroom, serenely untouched.

"This would be fine for a live-in manager, don't you think?" Maxine asked.

"Perfect."

They didn't say it would be perfect for Anna May, but they were both thinking it. Maxine was working up her courage to ask the girl if she'd be interested. It was a big step to make an offer that would change Anna May's life if she accepted, and Maxine was fully aware of the significance of her proposal.

"I don't know, Cora, maybe I shouldn't say anything to Anna May about managing this place. She's very young to take on so much responsibility. If she accepts, it might mean a break with her family, and I'd hate to be responsible for that."

"Now, Max, don't try to be the judge and jury about this. You have a reasonable job offer; you put it to Anna May, and then she makes up her own mind. As far as her youth goes, yes, she's young, but remember the training she's had at home. My house and yard have never looked better, and it seems to take her no time at all to keep them both immaculate. That girl knows how to work, and she's honest and personable. What more could you want?"

"Didn't I see her on the back of a motorcycle yesterday, hanging onto a sketchy-looking young man?"

"Well, you might have. That's Joey, but it's only temporary. He works at the county fair, which is over today. He'll be on his way to the next venue and probably the next girl."

"Will Anna May be sad to see him move on?"

"I think it's just been a bit of fun for her. A little walk on the wild side, but nothing serious. Maybe it's been good for her, who knows? She's such a serious little thing."

But the next day Anna May didn't come down for breakfast.

"She must be sleeping in," Mrs. Entwhistle said to herself, although that had never happened before. *She was probably out late last night with Joey. Hmmm, I can't remember hearing her come home.*

After a while, Mrs. Entwhistle climbed the stairs and stood outside the closed door to Diane's old room. She listened. No sound came from within. Delicately, she tapped. Nothing. She knocked louder, and called Anna May's name. When there was no response, she opened the door.

The bed had not been slept in.

Mrs. Entwhistle hadn't arrived at the age of eighty without knowing a few things. She understood the temptations of youth, especially when a youthful romance was faced with parting. Joey might have taken advantage of his imminent departure to convince Anna May to spend the night with him. It wasn't exactly a new story.

However, Anna May was in Mrs. Entwhistle's house and in her care. She felt a pulse of annoyance at being in a position of responsibility with no power. Anna May was an adult, albeit a very young and naive one, and she could do as she pleased. But it was with a shiver of dread that Mrs. Entwhistle contemplated having to explain all that to her mother.

Ordinarily, when faced with worrisome thoughts, Mrs. Entwhistle would scrub something, or weed something, or paint something. But Anna May had left her nothing to do. She walked aimlessly around her tidy house and yard looking for distraction. Roger accompanied her, his milky eyes fixed on her face. He didn't like it when she was restless.

She finally decided to bake cookies on the theory that a house perfumed with melting chocolate chips couldn't help but feel more cheerful. On this endless morning, she needed some cheer. She was taking the last batch out of the oven and thinking about what to have for lunch when she heard the Harley growl into her driveway. She stepped into the living room, parted the curtains and saw Anna May hop from the back of Joey's motorcycle. She unstrapped her helmet and handed it over without looking at him.

There didn't seem to be much conversation. In fact,

Joey seemed interested in the horizon. Anna May turned and walked rapidly toward the house. Mrs. Entwhistle hustled back into the kitchen. She didn't look up until Anna May cleared her throat.

"Oh, good morning. Well, I guess it's afternoon now," Mrs. Entwhistle said.

Anna May burst into tears.

Mrs. Entwhistle didn't say a word, just put some warm cookies on a plate, poured two glasses of milk and sat down at the table.

"I'm so sorry," Anna May said through sobs. "I've never done anything like that. I thought I loved him, and he was going away, and I let myself be talked into...No, *I* decided I wanted to be with Joey. I thought he loved me, and he said he wanted to work with the carpenters next week and learn how to do stuff so he could get a better job than with the carnival. I thought he meant all the things he said, but then this morning it became clear even to a domkop like me, that he, he...."

Mrs. Entwhistle interrupted her. "Anna May, don't tell me anything you'll later wish you hadn't. Least said, soonest mended. What you do is your business. If you think you made a mistake, well, I'm sorry, but there's not a person in this world who doesn't make 'em. Here, sit down and have a cookie."

~*~

Anna May seemed pensive the next day. She sighed as she gathered up the laundry; she stared unseeingly into the back yard as she washed the breakfast dishes; she startled when the doorbell rang, so lost in thought was she.

It was Maxine at the door, wearing a big smile and an air of determination. "Hi, Anna May, you're just the person I wanted to see."

"Don't you want Mrs. Entwhistle?"

"No, I'm here to talk to you," Maxine said, "although Cora can certainly join us. In fact, I hope she will."

"Good; I wouldn't miss this for anything," Mrs. Entwhistle said. "It sounds like a serious discussion that calls for the living room." She led the way.

When they were seated, Anna May looked from one face to the other. "Okay, what's going on?" she asked.

"First, I am so grateful to you for lining me up with your brother and his carpentry crew. The work is going so fast, I can hardly believe it. The inn finally seems like it will happen. You've been over, you've seen the work in progress," Maxine said.

"Yes. It's a mess now, but it's going to be wonderful."

"And my little house is almost ready, so I'll be moving in soon. My plan is that I'll come and cook breakfast for the B&B guests, but I don't want the day-to-day management of the inn." Maxine looked at Anna May expectantly, but received only a blank look in return.

"So, I wondered if you would be interested."

"Interested? In what?" Anna May's brows were furrowed as she tried to figure out what Maxine was getting at.

Mrs. Entwhistle cleared her throat meaningfully. Maxine was apt to tread so gently that no one could figure out what she was talking about.

"Managing the inn," Maxine said, taking the hint. "Living on the premises and handling the daily operations: keeping it clean, stocked, and inviting. Greeting the guests and checking them in. Keeping track of expenses and income. Helping with whatever needs doing to keep everyone happy. I guess." Maxine's voice trailed off. She wasn't too sure what the job entailed herself. "I can't afford to pay you very much at the start, but you'd have free room and board."

"But I'm only eighteen. I've never even been *in* a B&B, let alone run one."

Mrs. Entwhistle spoke up. "You have all the skills needed, honey. You know how to keep a place spotless, you can cook, and you're smart and personable and friendly. Guests would love you."

Anna May's head shook "no," at the compliments, but her eyes sparkled. "I don't know. It would mean staying here, not going back to my folks. Not being Amish anymore?"

"Certainly you could remain in your Amish faith, that's entirely up to you." Privately, Mrs. Entwhistle thought that the sight of Anna May in Amish garb would add to the B&B's charm, but she didn't say it. "It's a big decision, and you should give it serious thought, maybe talk it over with your parents. One thing to factor in, though, is that this decision isn't irrevocable. If you try it and don't like it, or if, after a while, you feel like you want to go home, then Maxine and I are perfectly capable of making a new plan."

"Don't let me talk you into anything," Maxine added. "You think about it. Take all the time you need. And if you decide it's not the job for you, I promise there will be no hard feelings. Not a single one." She smiled and patted Anna May's hand.

Chapter Eleven

Levi and his crew liked to start work at dawn and the first rosy streaks in the sky were accompanied by the pounding of hammers and the rasping of saws. Maxine was so worried about disturbing the neighbors she baked batches of brownies and took them door-to-door with her apologies.

"It's only for a week," she said, "I'm so sorry, but please just bear with me for a few days."

The men got an astonishing amount of work done, and before they quit for the day every tool was put away and every floor was swept. They all seemed to have a basic understanding of plumbing and electricity, but Maxine hired a plumber and an electrician to make sure the work met building codes. At noon, she, Anna, and Mrs. Entwhistle would lay out a feast, and the men would fall on the food.

"Apparently belching is considered okay," Mrs. Entwhistle observed in a whisper after the first meal.

"It's probably the only thing that enables them to move after all that eating," Maxine whispered back.

Levi heard them, though, and he laughed. "Yah, Amish burp," he said. "It means the food was good."

Mrs. Entwhistle liked Levi. He was a perfect house guest, cleaning up after himself meticulously and always appearing when something needed to go on the highest shelf or be carried up from the basement. It was hard to reconcile this Levi with the boy she'd seen falling into his mother's kitchen dead-drunk. She was dying to ask him if he was still on rumspringa, but she managed to restrain herself. It was none of her business.

Anna May felt no such constraint. "How about it, Lee? You still drinking and carrying on?"

They were sitting on the porch after supper. Bedtime came early, what with the dawn starts, but they took a few minutes to watch the autumn sun set. Mrs. Entwhistle pricked up her ears to hear Levi's answer.

"Nah, I'm done with that. I just got sick of it."

"That's what is supposed to happen with rumspringa," Anna May said, laughing. "You get sick of it and go back to Amish ways."

"That's what I'm gonna do," Levi said. "I'm seeing Adah again. She wouldn't go out with me while I was on rumspringa, never would ride in my car. Now I have to take the buggy to go see her."

Anna May knew Adah and didn't particularly like her, but she laughed at the thought of her wild brother trotting sedately off to court an Amish girl. "Will you be happy returning to Amish ways? You don't want to live your whole life feeling like you're missing out. And Adah will be strict about the rules, I think. Is that okay with you?"

"Well, I wish our lives could be different; more open. I like a lot about the English ways, but let's face it, I don't fit in with them. I never felt like myself dressed in their clothes or driving their cars. But when I'm Amish, I know where I belong. I know what to do and what to expect."

"Do you think you and Adah will get married?" Mrs. Entwhistle couldn't help asking.

"Yah, as soon as I join the church."

"Join the church? I thought all Amish were automatically in the church," Mrs. Entwisted said.

"No, that's something you decide as an adult. Once you make that choice, you are baptized, and then you are truly Amish, not just someone who was raised in an Amish home," Anna May clarified.

"Adah and I want our own place and to start a family," Levi continued. "There aren't any more farms left in the area for sale, but Pop said he'd give me five acres out by the road, enough for a barn, a pasture for the buggy horses and room for a big garden. We'll build the barn first and live in it while we save up to build a house. I can get work in one of the trailer factories. They pay real good, and Adah, she can stretch a dollar. Pretty soon I'll be a regular Amish guy with a big beard and a whole bunch of kids."

Levi sounded incredulous as he viewed his future.

"Is that what you really want, though?" Anna May asked.

There was a pause while Levi thought carefully of his answer. "It's for the best," he finally said. "I don't have your brains, Ammay. I have to be realistic about what I can do."

"I just want you to be happy." Anna May's voice was thick. "It was awful to see you in rumspringa. I was afraid you'd kill yourself. I'm glad you're not drinking anymore, but now, I don't know, I'm afraid you won't be happy staying Amish."

"I will be, I promise. It's a big relief to have made up my mind, actually. But what about you? Are you ready to go back home?"

Anna May struggled with how much to tell her brother. Finally, she decided to be honest.

"I don't think I'll be going back. The longer I'm away from the old ways, the farther away they feel. I miss Mom and Pop and the kids, and I miss home, but something in me just wants a different life."

"But how will you support yourself? You can't stay with Mrs. Entwhistle forever."

Mrs. Entwhistle realized they'd forgotten she was

there. She felt like an eavesdropper, but she didn't want to derail their talk by reminding them of her presence. Besides, she wanted to hear Anna May's answer. She sat as still as a stone.

"I have a job offer," Anna May said, "a pretty good one, I think. Maxine wants me to run the B&B when it's finished. I'd live there and take care of the guests, keep the place clean, help with cooking breakfast, do the shopping, keep the books. It sounds like a lot, but oh, Lee, I know I could do it! And I want to get my high school diploma and maybe even go on to college. I don't have a definite career in mind, but I think if I have a chance to study, it will become clear to me."

Levi nodded. "I guess I'm not too surprised. You liked school so much while the rest of us just went because we had to. If you want more school, I hope you can get it."

"What do you think Mom and Pop will do?" Anna May asked fearfully. "Do you think they'll shun me?"

"I can't speak for them," Levi said, "but I know for sure I won't. Yeah, they'll take it real hard to lose you, you know that. They've been so worried about me, they haven't spent much time worrying about you, and they'll blame themselves. Mom will think it's her fault for letting you make this visit. Pop will probably come and try to talk you into going home with him."

"I know. I expect that. I'll just have to face him, try to tell him my reasons and hope for the best."

~*~

The B&B was all but finished. Levi and the Amish carpenters packed up their tools and went home, leaving just a few loose ends like touching up paint and rearranging furniture. Anna May knew it was time to give Maxine her answer. The two of them were doing the final clean-up at the B&B. Anna May finished scrubbing the kitchen floor, emptied the mop bucket and pushed her hair out of her face.

"Maxine, could we talk?" she asked.

Maxine looked up with a smile. "Why, of course, honey. Are you going to put me out of my suspense?"

"Yes. I mean, yes, I'd like to be the B&B manager. I appreciate the opportunity, and I'll do everything I can to make it a success. I promise."

"Oh, great! I'm so pleased, Anna May. But are you sure? I don't want you to feel obligated. What about your parents? Have you talked to them about it? I'd hate to have them mad at me."

"I haven't talked to them yet, but that's what I'll do next. Honestly, I expect them to be upset. I'm trying to think how to say it so they'll know I'm serious and it's not just some sort of rumspringa thing."

"I'm sure they just want you to be happy."

"Oh, they do, but they want me to be happy in their ways, as an Amish girl, then as an Amish woman living the kind of life they think is right."

"Maybe you're underestimating them, Anna May. Maybe they have more insight into your character than you suppose."

"Maybe. I hope so."

~*~

"What are you going to call your B&B?" Mrs. Entwhistle asked. "Maxine's Merry Manor?"

Maxine made a gagging face. "Ick! Have you got any serious ideas?"

"Home Town Inn? Southern Comfort? Gober's Get-Away?"

"No, no, and no. Come on, you've got to have something better that that."

"Well, it was built by Amish carpenters, and will be managed by an Amish girl. What about the Amish Inn?"

"Oh, Cora, I love it, but do you think it would be disrespectful to sort of appropriate a different culture to name my place? I mean, I'd hate to insult Anna May or her community."

Mrs. Entwhistle smiled. "You've got the perfect person to ask about that."

But Anna May had her own troubles to consider. "Yeah, okay, I don't know," she said when asked.

"That's not very helpful," Maxine said.

"Sorry," Anna May said contritely. "I'm so worried about talking to my parents about staying here that I can't think of anything else."

Since Levi had gone back home with the carpentry

crew, Anna May had grown increasingly withdrawn. Her earlier chattiness was gone, and Mrs. Entwhistle actually missed it. She observed the dark circles under Anna May's eyes and knew she wasn't sleeping well. Despite Mrs. Entwhistle's resolve to mind her own business, she couldn't let the child suffer in silence.

"What's the worst thing about talking to your folks?" she asked.

"I guess it's not knowing when it will happen. Pop will just show up one day. There won't be a phone call or a letter telling me when to expect him. He'll just knock on the door."

Mrs. Entwhistle nodded. "Is there anything you could do to manage that uncertainty?"

"Like what?"

"You might seize the initiative, put it in a timeframe that works for you. That way, you'd be ready and maybe feel some control over the situation."

"You mean I'd knock on their door?" Anna May asked.

"Possibly."

"It's a long way to travel, and I don't know how I'd get there. Seltzburg is in the middle of nowhere. Would it be cowardly of me to break the news to them on the phone?"

"But your folks don't have a phone. How would you manage that?"

"I'd arrange a time to call with Levi, and he'd get them to the community phone."

Mrs. Entwhistle nodded thoughtfully. "If I may make a suggestion," she said.

"Please do," Anna May said.

"Write them a letter before you talk to them. You express yourself very well in letters, and it would give your folks time to think about their response."

"You're right," Anna May said. "They wouldn't have to respond right away to a letter; they could talk it over. That's what I'll do."

She spent the next couple of evenings bent over a pad of paper, drinking endless cups of tea, writing, crossing out, and rewriting her letter. Wadded-up balls of paper littered the floor around her chair. Sometimes, she'd have to go out and walk around the block to compose herself. Finally, she held out a couple of sheets of lined paper to Mrs. Entwhistle.

"Will you read it, please?"

"Of course."

Mrs. Entwhistle polished her glasses on her shirt tail and sat down at the table. She read:

Dear Mom and Pop,

I have decided to take a job as the manager of a Bed and Breakfast here, and will not be returning home. Maxine Gober, the lady who came to our house with Mrs. Entwhistle, is opening an inn, and she has offered me the position. I think it's a good opportunity for me to learn new skills, and I'm excited to try it. You know how I've always wanted to learn. I'm hoping to continue my education, finish high school and maybe even go to college. I'm not sure just how I'll manage all that, but I believe I can do it. The people here are kind, and I know they will help me all they can.

Mom and Pop, I will always be grateful for your love and the home you gave me growing up. I pray you'll understand that my choosing a different path in life won't change that. I'll always be your daughter. Tell my brothers and sisters that Anna May sends her love.

Your daughter,

Anna May

Mrs. Entwhistle folded the papers and gave them back to Anna May.

"Well? Is it okay?" Anna May asked anxiously.

"Yes, of course it is. I like the way you get right to the point without too much explanation, no excuses and no apologies. You are speaking from your heart, and that's apparent. I think it's good that you don't set any expectations for the future; that's up to them. Your folks may not interpret your words in just the way you want them to. Speaking as a mother, I think my first reaction would be to snatch you home as quickly as possible, and try to talk you out of any thoughts of leaving the Amish."

"That's what I'm afraid of. I don't want to argue with them."

"Yes, but we don't get to choose other peoples' reactions. Your parents will have to work through their feelings of guilt and disappointment in their own way. It may not go smoothly."

"I know. Is there anything I can do to make it better?"

"Keep reminding them that you love them and that you'll always be their daughter. Stay calm and focus on your goals. It's hard to imagine, I know, but this, too, shall pass. You want to get through it with your family relationship intact."

"I don't know if that's possible," Anna May sighed.

"If it isn't, then at least you'll be able to look back at your behavior and feel okay about it. You'll know you tried your best."

Chapter Twelve

Maxine shed some tears over all the possessions she had to let go when she moved to her tiny house, but once that part was over, she said she'd never felt so free.

"All those things," she said to Mrs. Entwhistle. "Why, I was a slave to them. I lived my life in service to *stuff*. And you know what? I broke one of the Spode plates today, and I wasn't even upset."

Maxine had followed Mrs. Entwistle's advice to use her best for everyday. Privately, Mrs. Entwhistle wondered if she'd given good counsel, but Max had the bit in her teeth now. She'd given all her everyday kitchenware to the charity shop and moved her precious china, silver and crystal into the limited cabinets of her miniscule kitchen.

"I think I'm going to love it here," Maxine continued, dipping a cookie into a paper-thin teacup.

"It looks like you already do," Mrs. Entwhistle observed, glancing around the room that contained the kitchen and sitting area.

Maxine's big house was decorated in burgundy, navy, and cream. The effect was luxurious and rich, but also a bit dark. This time, she'd chosen to go white. A slip-covered white love-seat and two blue and white ticking-striped spool chairs made up the seating in her living room. The cabinets in the kitchen were white, as were the backsplash, countertops and apartment-size appliances. For this autumn season, Maxine had scattered pillows and throws in colors of pumpkin, brown, gold and scarlet. The large windows looked out over trees blazing with the same colors.

"It does look nice, doesn't it?" Maxine said with satisfaction. "And in a month or so, I'll decorate for Christmas. It's just a matter of swapping out a few things."

Mrs. Entwhistle's holiday decorations were time-worn and of no particular theme. She still had the popsicle stick ornaments Diane and Tommy had made in elementary school, along with the paste and construction paper offerings from her grandchildren. She wouldn't have swapped them for Maxine's tasteful silver baubles, but she didn't see any reason to mention this. To each her own.

"Has Anna May heard from her folks yet?" Maxine asked, changing the subject.

"Not that I know of. I put the mail on the hall table every day and let her claim her own letters, but I haven't seen anything from home except for a few cards from her sisters. She's nervous about it, I can tell. Every day when she sees there's no letter from her parents, she visibly relaxes. However, we all know there will be a response sooner or later. She's trying to coordinate a phone call through Levi, but the parents aren't cooperating."

"I can't say that I blame them. It's a mighty big decision to be discussing in a phone call. Especially if you're not accustomed to using a telephone."

"I've tried to think if there's anything I could do to make it easier," Mrs. Entwhistle said, "but I think I should step back. This is a family matter. Don't you think?"

"I do," Maxine said firmly. "There are no words that will make Anna May's decision set well with her parents, so you might as well save your breath to cool your tea."

~*~

Levi tried. He talked to his parents time and again about connecting with Anna May via a phone call, but they weren't enthusiastic.

"Yah, sure, if you're used to talking on the telephone, it might be okay," Pop said. "But for Mom and me, we feel like we need to shout, and we can't hear what the other person is saying."

"Maybe less shouting," Levi suggested with a smile.

But Mom shook her head. "I ain't talking to Anna May about something this important until I see her in person. You tell her I said to come home."

"She don't want to, Mom. She hopes you won't make a big deal about it."

"Well, she should have thought of that sooner, because it *is* a big deal. When you decide to leave your home and your family and your religion..." Mom's voice went high and thin as she fought tears. "I think those two old ladies are behind this. Ammay never would have come up with this crazy plan on her own. I wish I'd never let them into this house."

"Now, Mother, calm yourself," Pop said.

"Calm myself? *Calm myself?*" Mom, predictably, became less calm by the second. "You sit there and tell me to be calm, but what are you doing about this daughter of yours who is going astray? You're the head of this family; it's up to you to stop her."

"Well, what do you think I should do?"

"I think we should go to her, talk to her, remind her of what she's giving up."

"She don't want that, Mom," Levi said again.

"I don't care what she wants." Mom's eyes flashed. "If she won't talk to us, then she can listen."

~*~

Moving day couldn't come soon enough for Anna May. Her stomach did flips when she thought that she'd be starting her job as Amish Inn manager. It felt like the first open door to the rest of her life, and she was filled with anticipation.

"Tomorrow," Maxine said in an evening phone call. "Tomorrow we get you moved in and settled. We've got plenty of time before we open."

Anna May ran to her bedroom to get ready. She was surprised to see how much her possessions had grown since she'd arrived. Dressing English sure did involve a lot of merchandise. She packed the suitcase she'd brought with her, and then had to borrow a couple of trash bags for the rest.

"Not a very glamorous way to arrive," she laughed, as she stowed her bags and hopped into Maxine's car for the short ride. Mrs. Entwhistle had been invited, but she said it should be a moment for Maxine and Anna May alone.

Maxine drove to the inn and paused in the empty street so they could take in the house's curb appeal. The old house glowed in the sunshine. It stood two stories high, painted bright white with black shutters and doors. Although the flowering shrubs and perennial borders were asleep for the year, the landscaping crew had trimmed and raked and edged so the dormant lawn was tidy. A small sign that Maxine had fashioned herself hung discreetly between two painted posts. "Amish Inn," it announced in a whisper. "Amish Inn."

"Do you think the sign should say more or be bigger?" Maxine asked anxiously. "Or should it have some kind of illustration on it, something Amish like a silhouette of a horse and buggy?"

"Yes," Anna May said. "An illustration of a horse and buggy would be worth a thousand words in telling what kind of inn it is."

Anna May had decided for herself that when there were guests, she'd wear white aprons over dark mid-calf dresses. That was her only concession to her roots. "I'd be more comfortable in jeans or sweats, but I want to look professional," she said, "and it doesn't hurt to give a nod to my background."

Inside, the house ticked quietly to itself. The big old grandfather clock in the hall could be heard all over the ground floor when the house was still. Maxine had always loved its metronomic sound. Like a heartbeat, she thought.

Anna May appreciated it, too. "That clock," she said. "The ticking reminds me of stitches in a quilt. Tiny, but strong enough to hold everything together."

"Why, Anna May, that's downright poetic!" Maxine said.

They deposited Anna May's things in the downstairs bedroom, then climbed the stairs together to inspect the guest rooms. Each was in perfect order, with starched white curtains at the windows, white duvets on the beds and white towels on the warming racks in the tiny *en suite* bathrooms.

"That's a lot of white," Anna May observed, "but it's more practical than it seems. I'll be able to bleach it if I need to."

Maxine gently stirred the bowls of potpourri, releasing the autumn scent of cinnamon. She adjusted a curtain here, and lace runner there. Finally, she stood still.

"I think it's beautiful. What do you think?"

"Why, same as you," Anna May said, her dimples appearing. "Now we just need some guests."

She didn't have to wait long, but how she wished those first guests had stayed home!

The first morning she woke in her new bedroom, she rose early. She'd adopted Mrs. Entwhistle's predilection for morning tea and was boiling the kettle when she heard a knock on the front door.

"Who can that be?" she said aloud. "Nobody's called for reservations, and who'd drop by at this hour?" She went to the door, tightening the belt of her bathrobe.

Her parents stood unsmiling on the stoop, with Levi making frantic faces behind them. Anna May felt herself go hot and cold. She was not prepared for this confrontation. She'd at least have liked to be dressed and ready for the day. But here they were, and there was nothing else to do but invite them in.

"Sorry, Ammay, sorry, I tried to call, but nobody answered at Mrs. Entwhistle's house," Levi whispered as he entered.

"I know, she misplaced her phone. She's been looking all over for it." Anna May cast a desperate look at her parents, who were settling themselves in the inn's front room. "Lee, what should I do?"

"You're going to have to face them sooner or later. Might as well be now," Levi said, edging back toward the door.

"Oh, no you don't," Anna May said, grabbing his sleeve and pulling him into the room. "You brought 'em, you stick around."

Her parents looked at her with carefully noncommittal faces. Levi was right. Ready or not, it was confrontation time.

"Mom, Pop, can I get you some coffee or tea? Have you had breakfast? I could make some eggs real quick."

"No," Pop said.

"We're not here to eat," Mom added.

With an inward call for courage, Anna May sat down opposite her parents. "I guess I know why you're here."

"We got your letter," Pop said, "but there was a lot left unsaid in it, important things that we didn't think should be discussed on the telephone." He paused and his eyebrows drew together in a straight line. "You are breaking our hearts, Anna May, and our rules."

Mom drew herself up and spoke. "Yah, but you're also making us real mad," she spat. "We trusted you—I trusted you—enough to let you make this visit, and this is how you repay us. Wait until the first chance you get, and run away from us and everything you've ever known!"

Anna May felt herself shrinking back into the little girl who feared and avoided Mom's wrath. She felt the hot red blush creeping up her neck and into her cheeks, the visible brand of her shame and agitation.

"I'm, I'm sorry, Mom. I hate to make you mad."

"Well, you should have thought of that before you sent that letter," Mom said. "I've about cried myself sick over that letter."

Mom cried? Anna May could have died on the spot. She'd never seen her mother in tears.

Pop stood. "Get your things," he said in a voice that brooked no disagreement. "You're coming home right now. We'll thrash all this out, but we'll do it at home."

"I can't," Anna May said in a small voice. "I work here now. Maxine is depending on me."

"Ach, Maxine!" Mom's voice dripped scorn. "Her and that Entwhistle woman, they led you away from us. You don't owe them nothing."

"It's not like that," Anna May protested. "They didn't influence me in any way; in fact, they said over and over that it was my decision alone."

"We'll see about that," Pop said. "Levi drove all night, and now we'll travel all day to get home. I need to get back as quick as I can. It's harvest time. Or did you forget that, too? And we're paying for the car by the day."

"I had to rent a car," Levi explained.

"Yah, more expense we didn't need," Mom added reproachfully. "The younger kids will have to do without something to make up for that cost. You go get your Amish clothes on so we can leave. You've caused enough trouble."

When she still hesitated, Pop rose to his full height. "Now, Anna May! We'll wait outside." He stalked to the door, followed closely by his wife.

Anna May had never heard her gentle Pop speak so coldly, as if he were speaking to someone he didn't like. Tears sprang to her eyes.

Shoulders slumped, she went to her bedroom. Rooting through one of the plastic bags, she found her Amish dress, stockings and shoes, but she couldn't find her bonnet anywhere. Mom would have a fit. Bonnets were hard to make and costly to buy. You just didn't lose one. Now the little kids would have to do without something else because of her.

Hurriedly, Anna May pulled on the thick black stockings and thrust her feet into the flat lace-up shoes. She fumbled with the straight pins that anchored her dress and apron, pricking her finger and fuming because only Amish men could have buttons on their clothing. It was one of the many things she never used to question that now seemed illogical. She twisted her hair into a low bun and pinned the sheer white covering over her head. Glancing in the mirror, she saw the old Anna May, drooping, crushed.

She was writing a note to Maxine when she heard the unmistakable growl of a Harley pulling up in front of the house.

Mrs. Entwhistle and the Amish Inn

Chapter Thirteen

Mrs. Entwhistle followed Joey at a discreet distance. When she'd heard his motorcycle, she'd dropped what she was doing and hopped on her scooter. She wasn't inconspicuous, but Joey seemed to pay no attention to his surroundings. He headed straight to the Amish Inn. Mrs. Entwhistle's heart raced. *What did he have in mind?* She pulled up behind Joey as he jumped off his bike, almost toppling it in his haste.

Anna May and her parents were on the front walk. Mrs. Entwhistle had to look twice to recognize Anna May. Not only was the girl wearing Amish clothing, her whole demeanor had changed. Instead of her usual upright posture, Anna May stared at the ground as she walked beside her father, who kept a tight grip on her arm.

Joey ran toward the family.

"Anna May? What are you doing with these people?

And why are you dressed like that? You look weird."

Anna May raised her head but she couldn't meet Joey's eyes. "I'm going home," she said softly.

"Are these your parents?" Joey asked.

"Just go on," Anna May said with more strength in her voice. "Go back to the fair or wherever you live. You've moved on, remember? This has nothing to do with you."

Pop spoke up. "Anna May is our daughter, and we're taking her back home with us. Who are you, young man?"

Joey ignored him. His gaze was fixed on Anna May's downcast face. "I came looking for you. I need to tell you something. Something important."

But the Bontragers continued to move *en masse* toward the SUV parked at the curb. Joey drew closer to Anna May, stepping in front of her father.

"Let go of her, old man," he snarled. "Don't make me hurt you."

Pop stopped walking and dropped Anna May's arm. He shook his head at Levi, who had moved forward with his fists bunched. "We don't believe in violence," he said, bowing his head humbly, "not even in self-defense. So if you want to hit me, you can go ahead."

Joey stared at him in amazement, unsure how to react to such an absurd invitation. Mrs. Entwhistle joined the little group, having taken it all in as she made her way across the yard.

"Mr. and Mrs. Bontrager, hello again," she said, a little out of breath. "Anna May, it looks like you're on your way home with your family, but I know they've had a long drive and soon will have another one. Please, won't you all come to my house and let me make you some breakfast? I find a trip always goes better if I start with a full stomach. I don't want you to leave our town hungry."

She smiled encouragingly at Mom, who glared back at her. Levi, however, perked up at the suggestion of breakfast.

"I sure could eat," he said, smiling at his former hostess. Having partaken of Mrs. Entwhistle's breakfasts while he stayed with her during the completion of the inn, he knew what he was in for.

Pop began shaking his head, but Mom surprised them all by overruling him. "Yah," she said, "we will come. I want to see where my girl has been staying."

She turned and marched to the car, not looking around to see if her family was following.

Mrs. Entwhistle touched Joey's arm. "You, too," she said. "Come and have something to eat, and we'll all get to know each other a little better."

But Joey shook off her touch. High on adrenaline and what he thought was love, he took an aggressive step toward Anna May. "C'mon," he said, grabbing her shoulder.

Levi and Mrs. Entwhistle sprang forward at the same moment. Levi's devotion to non-violence was forgotten as his fist shot out and connected, but not with his intended target. Instead, it was Mrs. Entwhistle's face.

~*~

Dr. Patel switched off the bright light he'd been shining in Mrs. Entwhistle's eyes.

"Looks okay," he said. "I don't see any damage to the eye, but I'd like you to be checked by an ophthalmologist just to be on the safe side. You really must stop getting into these fist fights!"

"Very funny," Mrs. Entwhistle said. "It was my own fault; I stepped into it. Levi would never hurt me on purpose."

"I think I'm supposed to report an assault to the police," Dr. Patel said.

"Heavens, no; don't do that! It was an accident. Levi meant to hit Joey, and he feels bad enough about getting me instead. I wouldn't dream of adding anything else to the burden that family is carrying."

The Bontragers never did have the breakfast she'd promised them. After her unfortunate encounter with Levi's fist, they'd gotten rather lost in the melee of people taking care of Mrs. Entwhistle. She lay on the lawn of the inn, unconscious and unaware that an ambulance had been summoned.

Later, she learned that Sanjay Patel had run across the street from his primary care practice to meet the ambulance. Delilah, Maxine, Shyam and Anjali arrived a few moments later, alerted by the lightening-like spread of bad news. It was a small town and everyone knew Mrs. Entwhistle.

She had vague memories of being placed on a stretcher, but she didn't really wake up until she was being transferred into a bed in the emergency department of the local hospital. Her friends surrounded her, but one face was missing.

"Where's Anna May?" Mrs. Entwhistle asked. Her voice sounded like somebody else's.

There was a collective throat-clearing and shuffling. Maxine said, "The Bontragers are out in the waiting room. They wanted to make sure you were all right before they went home."

"Hmm. Well, tell them I'm all right, and they can get on the road," Mrs. Entwhistle said. "I know they have a long drive ahead of them."

"Levi wants to see you before they go."

He entered the treatment room looking paler and more distressed than the patient. "Mrs. Entwhistle, I'm so sorry," he began, leaning down to look in her eyes. "You know I'd never hit you or hurt you in any way. I was aiming for that creep with the bike."

"Yes, Levi, I know you were. I'm fine. Don't give it another thought. Well, maybe you might spare a thought or two about impulse control; that wouldn't hurt. But please don't worry; I'm fine. You need to get your family back home. Is Anna May okay about going with you?"

"Uh, well, she...."

"Anna May is on her way," Maxine said mysteriously.

Mrs. Entwhistle closed her eyes. Nothing made sense, but she couldn't figure it out at the moment. An ominous drumbeat was beginning in her temple, and it took all of her attention.

~*~

Anna May's last glimpse of her family was a huddled group of black-clad people gathered like a flock of crows around an inert object on the lawn. No, not a flock. What was the phrase? A murder of crows.

Then she had to hang on tight to Joey's waist as he made the big bike jump forward. Anna May's head covering flew off and fluttered behind her like an ectoplasm. What was she doing? What should she be doing instead? But thoughts refused to take shape. She simply followed the path of least resistance led by Joey. That she'd left her friend and mentor stretched out unconscious on the ground seemed so ludicrous as to be simply untrue. She couldn't wrap her mind around it.

Joey didn't try to speak above the rushing wind. He concentrated on driving, and Anna May concentrated on hanging on. There was no helmet for her, and she was aware of the softness of her head versus the hardness of the pavement beneath them. When Joey slowed for a stoplight, she shouted, "Where are we going?"

"I'm taking you away," Joey answered, and they were off again.

It seemed like hours, but Anna May knew her senses were not reliable. Finally, Joey turned off onto an unpaved road completely overhung by trees. He coasted to a stop in front of a small travel trailer set off by itself in the middle of an empty field. "We're here," he said.

"But where? Is this yours? Is this where you live?"

"Yeah, it's mine," Joey said. He was trying to act nonchalant, but she heard the pride in his voice. "I saved up and bought it myself, just got it a couple days ago. Man, it was dirty, but I cleaned it up good. Now I can take my home wherever I go."

"How? You can't pull it behind the bike."

"Yeah, well, I've got a line on trading the bike in for a truck. C'mon in."

The tiny space was worn, but immaculate. It smelled of soap and fresh air. Joey opened drawers and hidden storage compartments with housewifely pride, showing Anna May around although neither of them could move more than six steps in any direction.

"It's really nice, Joey," Anna May said. "You've done a good job. I can tell this is your home now."

"Yeah, first one I ever had. Dad and I usually just stay with the carnival when we're on the road, and then in the winter at his place in Florida, but, well, that's *his* place. This is mine."

"Don't you miss being with your Dad?"

"No. Do you miss being with yours?"

The question caught Anna May off-guard, and she

was surprised to find herself in a flood of tears. "I shouldn't be here. My folks will never get over this."

"What's with your family, anyway? Why are you dressed like that? You look medieval or something."

"We're Amish, Joey. I told you that."

"Yeah, but it didn't really register. Before you looked and acted just like everybody else. Well, better than most, but you know what I mean."

Anna May smiled weakly at Joey's attempt at a compliment. He certainly had rough edges, but it was no wonder, considering his upbringing. She'd never expected to see him again after their last parting, but he'd swooped in like Sir Galahad and carried her out of what he perceived to be a bad situation. Now neither of them knew quite what to do with themselves or each other.

"I have to go back," she said. "Mrs. Entwhistle got hurt somehow. I didn't see what happened."

"I did. Your brother slugged her."

"Levi? He wouldn't do that."

"No, he was aiming at me. Your Dad said Amish people didn't fight, and then your brother threw a punch. What the hell?"

"I'm sure Levi just lost his temper. We really don't fight or return violence. But poor Mrs. Entwhistle! I've got to see if she's all right."

"Oh, yeah, she's all right; you can count on it. Old ladies like her are tough as Army boots."

"But she was on the ground! Please take me back, Joey."

"What if your folks are still there? They were trying to get you to go back to the farm with them, weren't they? And I could tell you weren't happy about it."

"I don't know what happened. I got mixed up for a while," Anna May admitted. "Pop was so sure of himself, and I've always obeyed him. When he and Mom told me to get my Amish clothes on and come with them, I couldn't *not* do it."

"Is that what you want, though?"

"No! Yes. I don't know. I've got a job managing Maxine's bed and breakfast, and I'm excited about that. I want to go to school, get my high school GED and go on to college. But I feel so guilty about making my folks unhappy. I don't know what to do."

"You want to go to school? Geez, I couldn't wait to drop out. Well, whatever. Look, why don't you stay with me until you figure things out? The carnival leaves tomorrow. Just ride along. It'll be fun. You can probably get a job helping out on the midway. They always need people at the concessions stands."

"But my job...and Mrs. Entwhistle. My folks must be so worried. I can't just disappear."

"Look, that B&B place isn't even open yet. Call the owner, explain, check on the old lady, whatever it takes to settle your mind. Your folks will be okay. You're an adult. You can try a different kind of life."

Anna May thought there were a lot of holes in Joey's

reasoning, but she felt so tired all she wanted to do was sleep. She'd let him carry the burden of decision-making for now.

~*~

Mrs. Entwhistle pooh-poohed the idea that she be admitted to the hospital overnight for observation.

"Maxine can observe me," she said. "Besides, I've got to get home to Roger. He needs his supper and he's used to sleeping on my bed at night. I don't want to get him all upset. He's old."

"Well, my dear Mrs. E., so are you," Dr. Patel pointed out with a smile that softened his customary brusque bedside manner. "We want to make sure there is no brain swelling from that punch you took."

"You gotta have a brain for it to swell," Mrs. Entwhistle said, "and anybody who steps between two angry young men clearly doesn't have one. This is what I get for poking my nose into other peoples' business. No. I'll go on home now, and maybe I can talk Max into spending the night with me. Doesn't that sound okay?"

Dr. Patel reluctantly agreed, with the stipulation that he'd stop by to check on her himself after work. Maxine drove her sporty red car around to the discharge door and took Mrs. Entwhistle home.

Maxine, for once, was caught short without her usual stockpile of homemade soup. "I just haven't had time to make any," she confessed, "what with moving and getting the inn ready to open. Oh, Cora, what am I going to do about the inn? I don't know where Anna

May has gone or when she'll come back. *If* she'll come back."

Before Mrs. Entwhistle could rally her aching brain to formulate a reply, the door opened and Anjali Patel appeared. She wore a bright sari, and her face was full of love and concern.

"Ladies, oh, poor ladies!" she crooned.

Mrs. Entwhistle remembered the same concern expressed in the very same words after she and Max had been in a car wreck. Anjali and Shyam had come to their rescue then, and it looked like history was repeating itself.

"Look," she said, nodding at the covered dish in her hands, "I bring butter chicken and naan. You eat, you will feel better," Anjali said. She went directly to the kitchen and proceeded to set the table and dish up the food she'd brought. "Come, you eat now."

Mrs. Entwhistle's stomach contracted at the thought of food, and her head spun dizzily when she stood, but she wouldn't have hurt her friend's feelings for anything. And sure enough, after a few bites her stomach relaxed and her head agreed that food was a good thing. She cleaned her plate.

"No. No more, thank you. That was perfect. It was just what I needed," she said.

Maxine, however, still had a full plate in front of her.

"You do not like it?" Anjali said.

"Oh, no. It's not that. You know I love your food," Maxine said. "I'm just so upset. The inn is almost

144

ready to open, but now Anna May has gone off with that boy, and I don't know what I'm going to do. I hoped to have a soft opening just before the holidays, and Anna May was going to make sure everything was ready and write some ads for the *Pantograph* to run. But now...."

Anjali smiled at her friends tenderly. "Why, you have no worries, my poor lady. I will get the inn ready, and if Anna May is not back by the time you wish to open, I will be in charge."

"You? Oh, no, Anjali, that is too kind, but you are busy helping Shyam with the tiny house village," Maxine protested.

"Shyam does not need my help anymore," Anjali said proudly. "He has made such a good recovery from his stroke that I hardly see him during the day, he is so busy. Look, I am an inn-keeper. Remember, Shyam and I were proprietors of the Patel Paradise for many years. I do not know much, but I know how to run an inn."

"But you have a life, too," Maxine protested. "I can't let you give it up for me."

"Let us think logically," Anjali said. "If you open the inn for Christmas, you will certainly have guests. But in January and February? I doubt it. People do not visit small towns like ours in the doldrums of winter. When warm weather returns, then your inn will be busy. But that is several months away, is it not? And we are faced with a tiny little emergency right now, today. And the solution for today's little tiny emergency is: Me."

Chapter Fourteen

Levi was never so happy to get out of a car. Very few words had been spoken during the drive home, but the tension was palpable. Mom and Pop had watched open-mouthed as Anna May climbed on the back of Joey's Harley. When she'd roared off with that boy, Levi had expected some kind of matching explosion from his parents, but instead, their words dried up. Mom's mouth was a thin line; Pop's eyes were like two gray stones. Whatever they were feeling, it stayed inside.

After they received assurance that Mrs. Entwhistle was not badly hurt, they'd ordered Levi to take them home. They exited the car and entered the house without a word. Levi carried in the few things they'd taken, then went to the barn where Jacob was finishing up the milking.

"Hi! Where's Ammay?" Jacob asked, wiping his

hands on a gunny sack. "She in the house?"

"She didn't come home with us," Levi said.

"She didn't? I thought that was why you went. To bring her back."

"Yeah, well, she didn't see it that way."

"What happened?"

"I'll fill you in, but first I gotta take the rental car back or we'll get charged for another day. I need you to come get me in the buggy."

"I ain't had supper yet," Jacob said.

"I'll get you a hot dog at Dairy Queen," Levi said.

"Okay, then," Jacob said with a grin. "And on the way home, you can tell me what happened with Ammay."

"Wish I could. Wish I knew."

As they jogged home in the buggy, Levi tried. "She wasn't the same, Jake. We got there real early in the morning, and Ammay was still in her nightclothes when she came to the door. I wouldn't hardly have known her with her hair all down, she looked so different. Then Mom and Pop made her get her Amish clothes back on, and she looked more like herself, but she didn't seem the same."

"Were Mom and Pop mad?" Jacob asked apprehensively. None of the children had ever seen their parents really angry. It was an unsettling thought.

"Mom was; Pop just acted...I don't know, cold, I guess would be the word. He didn't say much, but

Ammay got the message right away. She kind of drooped like the garden does when it's dry. She was coming home with us, although I could tell she didn't want to. But she didn't have the nerve to defy Pop. We were actually walking out to get in the car when this guy came riding up on a Harley, a big old bike, and said Ammay should come with him. He grabbed her."

"What did you do?" Jacob's eyes were huge.

"I took a swing at him. Only Mrs. Entwhistle stepped right in front of him, and I hit her instead. Geez, she had to go to the hospital in the ambulance." Levi's voice broke. "I never meant to hurt her. I like that old gal. I didn't even realize I was swinging until my fist connected with her face. I feel terrible about it."

"What did Ammay do?"

"She got on the back of the guy's bike and rode away with him."

"Ach du lieva! She just left? What did Pop do?"

"He didn't have much choice. We got in the car and came home. It was a long ride, let me tell you."

"Is Ammay going high? Do you think we'll have to shun her?" Jacob asked. Anna May was his favorite sister; his head felt hot and tight when he thought of never seeing her again.

"Don't know." Levi shook his head. "I don't know what to expect next."

~*~

Mrs. Entwhistle had a headache that just wouldn't quit. In fact, it seemed to be getting worse. Roger stuck by her side, trying his best to lick her red, swollen eye.

"I'm okay, Rog," Mrs. Entwhistle said over and over, but the little dog wasn't buying it.

When Dr. Patel stopped by on his way home from work, he didn't buy it, either. "I don't like the looks of this," he said, shining a pencil light in Mrs. Entwhistle's eye. "Follow my finger." He moved it to the left and right.

Mrs. Entwhistle dutifully moved her eyes, but that finger was tricky, and she couldn't keep track of it.

"How many fingers am I holding up?

"Um, two? No, one."

Dr. Patel switched off his pen light and put it back in his pocket.

"You have a concussion," he said, "and there may be some brain swelling. It will probably resolve within a couple of days, but I think you should be monitored tonight. I must insist that you spend the night in the hospital."

"Oh, no, that's not necessary," Mrs. Entwhistle said. She tried to make her voice sound strong, but it didn't, not even to her own ears. "And besides, what about Roger?"

"Roger is coming home with me," Dr. Patel said. "You know he'd like nothing better than to sleep on JJ's bed tonight."

It was true that Roger loved JJ. The little boy and his mother, Delilah, had lived with Mrs. Entwhistle for a time, and it was the beginning of a lifelong friendship between boy and dog. Despite his advanced years, Roger wiggled all over like a puppy when he saw JJ.

Mrs. Entwhistle knew her dog would have a happy night. She wasn't so sure about herself, but she believed there was no point in consulting a doctor if you didn't follow directions. So she allowed herself to be loaded into Dr. Patel's car, driven to the hospital, and admitted.

"We're out of private rooms in Neurology, hon," the admitting clerk said. It was a small hospital, after all.

And so it was that Mrs. Entwhistle found herself bunking in with a lady even older than herself. Mrs. Klepper was delighted to have a roommate.

"Been here for two days with nobody to talk to," she said, as soon as Mrs. Entwhistle was settled in the adjoining bed. "I had this real bad headache, oh, it was just a'hammerin' and a'poundin', and maybe I had a little stroke, they're not sure, so here I am. I been here a couple days, so I'm like an old hand. I can show you the ropes; which nurses are good and which ones to look out for. I can tell you what food to order, and, and...well, I guess that's about all we get to choose."

Mrs. Entwhistle smiled politely. Her headache had been aggravated by all the moving around, and she wanted nothing more than to close her eyes and be still.

But Mrs. Klepper wasn't deterred by her roomie's lack of conversation. "Now if you want something during the night, you just push that there button, but don't expect nobody to come a'runnin'. Far as I can tell, they don't run around here unless somebody's about to croak. So you punch that button a good half-hour ahead of when you'll need something.

"And if you have visitors, just have 'em pull that curtain around your bed. It's supposed to be more private-like, but to be honest I gotta tell you I'll still hear every word that's said. Just so's you know."

Mrs. Entwhistle sighed.

"And about the TV. Now, I like to watch them Hallmark movies. They've already started running some of the Christmas ones. I like a good romance around a Christmas tree, don't you? Although it sure makes me sad to think of my Elmer. He's been gone for many a year now. Died just real sudden during the night. I woke up the next morning, and I was layin' there beside a corpse. Well, it makes a body jump up real quick, I can tell you."

Mrs. Entwhistle fluttered her fingers in what she hoped would be taken for a time-out signal.

Undaunted, Mrs. Klepper talked on. "I never heard a thing when Elmer passed, he just went so gentle, but it's made me feel spooky at night, him going like that. I leave the TV on all the time now. It's nice to have something to look at if I wake up, which I usually do. We old folks don't sleep like we used to, do we? My mama used to say, 'Now that I've got the time to sleep, I cain't.' Myself, I wake up early every dang morning. Ain't much to do at four a.m., especially in here, so TV comes in handy. I'll keep the sound turned real low, though, so it won't bother you. If it does, you just say so, okay?"

Mrs. Entwhistle said, "Mm." She closed her eyes.

"Did you bring your nightgown and stuff from home? They put you in one of them Johnnys but your rear end hangs out for all the world to see. Wouldn't be surprised if they don't walk you down the hall like that on purpose and them all just laughing behind their hands. Now, if you ain't got your robe with you, put on another Johnny backwards. At least that'll keep you decent. Oh, and you can forget about getting a bed bath. That's a thing o' the past. Maybe they'll let you take a shower, but not in private."

"I think I'll go home in the morning," Mrs. Entwhistle said faintly. "So I won't need to worry about bathing here."

"Well, that's as may be, I hope you're right about that. This is no place a person wants to linger."

Mrs. Klepper raised herself on one elbow and took a good look at Mrs. Entwhistle's face. "Say, what happened to you, anyways? You sure got a shiner. Did you fall?"

"No, I got in a fight," Mrs. Entwhistle said. She pitched her voice at a low growl, disregarding the pain it sent through her head. "You should see the other guy. He just wouldn't stop talking. I can't abide a person who won't shut up."

Mrs. Klepper raised her eyebrows and shut her mouth. Wonderful peace reigned in the small room. Mrs. Entwhistle slept.

In the morning, she felt much better. She had no problem identifying how many fingers Dr. Patel was holding up, and declared herself ready for discharge.

"But I want you to rest," Dr. Patel said sternly.

Maxine entered the room in time to hear that. "She will, I'll see to it."

"I mean really rest," Dr. Patel continued. "No working in the yard, no cooking, no washing dishes, no walking Roger. Got it?"

"Got it," Mrs. Entwhistle said.

"Double-got it," Maxine added. "I'll take her home and put her to bed, and then I'll go by your house and pick up Roger."

But Mrs. Entwhistle resisted the idea of being put to bed. She said she'd rather bunk on the sofa. "It's boring up in my room alone," she said. "Here, I can watch TV if I want to, or look out the window, or smell what's cooking. What is cooking, anyway?"

"Baked potato soup," Maxine said. "I made it this morning, and I must say, I think it's one of my better batches."

Mrs. Entwhistle's mouth watered. The hospital breakfast had left a lot to be desired. "Could we eat early?"

"Of course, but guess what else I brought? My

cinnamon rolls!"

Mrs. Entwhistle moved to get up, triggered by the thought of cinnamon rolls, but Maxine waved her back down. "You just stay put. I'll bring you one with a cup of tea."

Mrs. Entwhistle settled back on the cushions. Once Roger came home, her world would be right again. Then she could go back to worrying about Anna May. But for now, she'd follow the doctor's orders.

~*~

Anna May felt trapped in the travel trailer. She'd cleaned the already-clean surfaces and taken stock of the dinky kitchen.

"Not room to swing a cat," she muttered to herself.

Joey had been gone all day yesterday and would be gone all day today, helping to strike the midway and get the carnival ready to move on to the next venue. His hoped-for pickup truck deal fell through, and he'd had to make towing arrangements with one of the carnie roustabouts who had a truck. He grumbled about the cost, but Anna May thought he was secretly pleased to be keeping his Harley at least for now. Joey insisted that Anna May stay out of sight.

"We don't want too many people to know you're here just yet," he said. "Don't want to deal with a bunch of questions. When we get settled in the next place, you'll be with me, and nobody will think anything of it."

Anna May got the feeling that nobody would think anything of it because they'd seen it before, Joey showing up with a girl. Her face grew hot at the thought of the conclusions that would be drawn about her. To stop feeling that feeling, she scrubbed the floor again.

Eventually, even she could find nothing else to do. She sat on the trailer's step and looked at the trees. They reminded her of the ones that lined the lane at home. The cows would come plodding up that lane in the early dusk. They knew when it was milking time. They swished their tails and bobbed their heads peacefully. The collie, unimaginatively named Shep, followed at their heels, but they didn't need to be herded. The warm, earthy smell of cattle would fill the barn as she and Levi and Jacob did the evening chores. Sometimes, Anna May rested her forehead on the cow's rough flank, almost dozing as she milked. The barn cats and Shep stood close by, ready in case anyone felt like shooting a stream of warm milk into their mouths.

When the chores were finished, Mom would have supper ready. The little kids would be setting the table in the kitchen, chattering like birds. Pop would stomp his feet on the mat outside the door and swoop up the baby, tossing him in the air until he shrieked with laughter. Then they'd all sit down around the table and join hands. Everyone would get quiet and bow their heads in silent grace. After a minute, Pop would say, "Amen."

In her mind's eye, she saw food being passed from

hand to hand. The baby often sat in Anna May's lap and ate from her plate. There was plenty to eat, none of it fancy, all of it homegrown. For dessert, Mom might open one of the golden jars of peaches she'd preserved. There was no hurry. When everyone was finished, they'd join hands and bow their heads again until Pop said amen.

Maybe she wouldn't be welcome at that table ever again. Maybe that baby brother would grow up without knowing her. Her throat closed and her breath caught as she thought of what she was losing.

Chapter Fifteen

Mrs. Entwhistle felt fully recovered. "Just a tempest in a teacup," she said to Maxine. "I don't know why Sanjay felt he had to make such a big deal of it."

"He probably doesn't have too many eighty-year-old patients who get punched in the eye and knocked unconscious," Maxine said.

"Well, still. I *told* him I was fine."

In fact, Mrs. Entwhistle was itching to do something she believed needed to be done. Restless energy radiated from her in waves.

"I've got to find Anna May and talk to her about what's going on," she said. "We don't know if she's safe and happy, or staying with Joey because she can't think what else to do. Knowing her, I bet she's ashamed to face us after what happened. She takes everything to heart and blames herself."

"But we have no idea where she could be," Maxine pointed out. "The fair left town and who knows where they went next."

"I wonder if Sheriff Martinez could find out for us. He probably has access to all kinds of information."

But the sheriff couldn't help them. "We don't keep track of legitimate businesses for no reason," he said.

Next, Mrs. Entwhistle asked her great friend, Pete Peters, Deputy U.S. Marshal.

"You know I'd do anything for you," Pete said. He'd never forgotten that Mrs. Entwhistle saved his life by performing CPR after he got shot. "But I can't use the Federal data base for personal use. Besides, we don't even know the name of the carnival company."

That was an easy fix. Mrs. Entwhistle knew a guy—she almost always did—in town government. One phone call to Permits revealed that the carnival was called Mid-American Amusements. The Internet provided the information that their next stop was in a town twenty miles away.

"Let's go. If we see Joey, we'll at least be able to find out if Anna May is with him. It gives us a place to start. Of course, you'll have to drive," she said to Maxine.

Having a scooter as her sole means of transportation had its disadvantages. Maxine was always ready to drive her sporty red car, but this time there was a problem.

"I don't think the carnival opens until evening on weekdays," Maxine said, "and lately I can't see very well at night. I'd be hesitant to drive us after dark."

Mrs. Entwhistle couldn't see to drive at night either. It reminded her of a joke, which she immediately told.

"So there was this old guy who was popular with the ladies despite being rude, fat, and obnoxious. 'What do you see in him? Why do you put up with him?' they were asked. The ladies shrugged and answered with one voice: 'He can see to drive at night.'"

They shared a gentle laugh. "Too bad we don't know him," Maxine said.

"But we do know Pete. I'm going to ask him if he'll take us."

Pete quite predictably dropped everything to accommodate them, and late afternoon found them in his car being safely driven to the carnival site. He even insisted on buying them each cotton candy when they arrived.

"We're not here as fair-goers," Mrs. Entwhistle protested.

"Yeah, but I think it's a Federal law; you have to eat cotton candy if you're at a fair," Pete said, dead-pan.

"Well, okay, then."

They walked the mid-way slowly, peering into every booth and concession stand, but they didn't see Joey or Anna May. Mrs. Entwhistle spied a cinder-block building marked Restrooms.

"I've got to wash this cotton candy off my hands," she said, climbing the steps to the door marked Women.

When she opened the door, she came face to face with Anna May. They both gasped and fell back, which caused Mrs. Entwhistle to teeter alarmingly on the top step. Anna May instinctively reached out to steady her. The next minute they were embracing.

"Oh, Anna May, I've been so worried about you," Mrs. Entwhistle said, rocking slightly.

"I'm sorry. I'm sorry. I know I've caused all kinds of trouble. I'm not welcome anywhere now, and it's my own fault."

"Not welcome! Why, child, you're *always* welcome at my house, and Maxine's, too. That's why we're here: to find you and make sure you haven't forgotten that. Are you staying with Joey?"

Anna May turned a deep shade of red. "I know it's wrong to be with him like this. I just didn't know what else to do."

By now, Maxine had joined them and they were creating a traffic jam at the restroom door. Mrs. Entwhistle led them over to where Pete stood waiting.

"Pete, looky here who I found. Anna May, this is Pete Peters, a real good friend of mine."

Anna May shook hands shyly. "Pleased to meet you," she said to her shoes. But Pete was having none of that. He spoke with his customary directness.

"Hi, Anna May. A friend of Mrs. Entwhistle's is my friend, too. We came to find you today to see if you're happy and if you want to stay where you are. You say the word, and we'll get lost."

Anna May shook her head. "Please don't get lost."

"Then you'd better tell us what we can do for you."

Anna May motioned to a picnic table set behind the tents for the carnival workers. No one was using it, so they had a modicum of privacy. She began to talk.

"I've been thinking a lot since I left. Ran away. That was wrong of me." She held up her hand to stop Mrs. Entwhistle's protestations. "No, it was. I'm ashamed that I left you lying there on the ground, left my parents standing there not knowing what to do. I acted like a coward. I'm so sorry."

Mrs. Entwhistle nodded. She knew not to speak.

Anna May continued. "Being with Joey is like a time-out. I don't have to make any decisions. Nobody cares what I do or don't do, how I dress, whether I'm Amish or high. I didn't realize how much pressure I was feeling until it was lifted. I think I'd like to stay for a while."

"How long a while?" Maxine asked.

"I don't know yet. I'm leaving you in the lurch with the inn, and again, I'm so sorry. I've never in my life been undependable, but I am now."

"Don't worry about the inn," Maxine said. "Anjali Patel has offered her help. And if we don't open by Christmas, the world won't end. You just do what you have to do to be healthy and happy."

"What about your parents?" Mrs. Entwhistle asked. "You owe them more than to leave them wondering and worrying about you."

"You're right, but I'm afraid they're going to worry and wonder no matter what I do. I'll write to them and tell them I'm safe and well. That's really all I know at the moment."

"Will you give them a way to get in touch with you?"

"No. I'm not ready for that."

"What if they ask me where you are?" Mrs. Entwhistle said. "I won't lie."

"I'm not asking you to," Anna May said. "It won't be a lie to say you don't know where I am, because you won't. If you want to say you've seen me, or give them the name of the carnival company, that's okay. You have to do what you think is right."

"I feel a lot of empathy for your family," Mrs. Entwhistle said sternly. "They love you, and they're worried."

"I hate that, but right now I can't help it."

Maxine tugged gently on Mrs. Entwhistle's sleeve. "Let's let Anna May make her own decisions," she said gently. "All parents worry; you and I have worried plenty about our children. It goes with the territory. This family will work it out, just as we did."

Mrs. Entwhistle relaxed and smiled at Maxine appreciatively. She could always count on Maxine to tactfully remind her to back off.

~*~

The Amish Inn received its final tweaks from the able hands of Anjali Patel. For several days, she arrived in the morning and with effortless simplicity, did what needed to be done. Then the big house stood empty, holding its breath, waiting for whatever would happen next.

Maxine, happy in her new little nest, held her breath, too. What if this had all been an epic mistake? She really couldn't afford to have the inn stand empty and idle; she was counting on it to bring in some income, at least enough to pay for its own taxes and utilities. She found herself in the uncomfortable position of supporting two dwellings on a retirement income. But advertising a grand opening seemed beyond her capabilities.

Not so with her best friend. Mrs. Entwhistle could scarcely contain herself. Maxine was feeling overwhelmed, Mrs. Entwhistle understood that, but the hard work was done. To her, it seemed all that remained was to run a couple of ads, unlock the front door and wait for the guests to pour in. Mrs. Entwhistle decided to have a talk with her old friend and former boss, the editor of the town newspaper, the *Pantograph*.

Jimmy Jack McNamara had struggled with tendencies toward indolence, ignorance and indecision his whole life. When he hired Mrs. Entwhistle to be his town beat reporter, she uncovered a money-laundering scheme involving the president of the high school Booster Club. The resulting scandal had the whole town grabbing eagerly for copies of the *Pantograph* which shook the editor out of his comfortable lassitude. He'd never been the same.

He viewed Mrs. Entwhistle warily as she entered his office and plopped down in the modernistic and supremely uncomfortable chair opposite his desk.

"Whooee," Mrs. Entwhistle said, fanning herself with her hand. "I can't believe it's so warm this late in the year. That humidity just takes it out of a person, doesn't it?"

"Good morning," Jimmy Jack said nervously. "What can I do for you?" He'd learned it was best to get right down to it. Otherwise, no telling where the conversation might go.

"Well, I came to ask your advice," Mrs. Entwhistle said with a disarming smile.

Jimmy Jack felt his shoulder muscles tighten. No matter what he said, this wasn't going to end well.

"See, Maxine is ready to open her bed and breakfast inn, but Anna May, the Amish girl she'd hired to run it, has, well, she's taking some time off."

"She's taking time off before she even starts her job?" Jimmy Jack asked.

"It's complicated. Point being, Max is kind of stuck at the moment. She's moved into her tiny house, so she's making a big adjustment there, and you know we old folks sometimes aren't real adaptable."

Jimmy Jack knew better than to agree or disagree. He maintained a neutral expression.

"So, I'd like to help her get this thing off the ground. Originally, she wanted a soft opening during the Christmas holidays. Do you have any ideas about how we can make that happen?"

Jimmy Jack blinked. "Well, I haven't thought about it," he said. "I'd have to, um, give it some thought."

"I think a feature article in the *Pantograph* would be helpful, don't you?"

"Oh, sure, no problem. Maxine said she wanted to run some ads, too, but I told her to spread her net wider than the hometown paper. She wants to attract out-of-towners. So I think she could utilize the Internet, social media and all that."

"We don't know how," Mrs. Entwhistle said simply.

"I wish I could help with that, but I'm not a computer whiz, either." Jimmy Jack paused, and then his face brightened. "You know who is? Dex Schofield!"

"Dex! You're right; that boy can flat make a computer sit up and sing. But he's so busy. They've got the new baby and all, and his job with the Washington Post keeps him hopping."

"It wouldn't hurt to just talk to him about it, though, would it? Dex is like greased lightening on the computer, and he could talk you through it over the phone. He wouldn't have to leave home."

Mrs. Entwhistle wondered why she hadn't thought of that herself. She still missed Dex. He'd been an intern at the *Pantograph* when she was a reporter, and together they'd done some first-rate investigative journalism. They'd been celebrities for a minute, resulting in Dex being recruited by the Washington Post before he even graduated from college. He and his wife, Lara, and their new baby boy lived in D.C. now, but Mrs. Entwhistle tele-talked with Dex at least once a week. It was one of her chief regrets that baby Thomas wasn't within cuddling distance.

"Much as I'd love to have them visit, I know their lives are too busy right now. But maybe Dex could help remotely," she said. "I'll give him a call."

That evening she sat before her phone beaming at the images of Dex, Lara, and sleeping baby Thomas on her screen. Dex had been hearing all about Maxine's new business venture as it evolved, so he didn't need much bringing up to speed. When Mrs. Entwhistle broached the idea of online advertising, he was enthusiastic. Unfortunately, his advice was given in a foreign language. Mrs. Entwhistle stared at him hopelessly while he spouted terms she'd never heard of.

"Is Maxine on Facebook?" Dex finally asked.

"Yes, I think so. She often mentions seeing things that Geraldine's doing in Australia, and I guess that's where she'd see them."

"Okay, she can run Facebook ads. Does she have a lot of Facebook friends?"

"Why, I have no idea. How would a person know?"

"You can see how many friends you have and who they are in a box at the side of the screen. You just click on Friends. Does Max use e-mail a lot?"

"Again, I know she e-mails Geraldine."

"She needs to set up a group e-mail of all her contacts. Then she can send out blasts to keep the inn at the top of peoples' minds."

Dex went on. Foreign terminology floated in and out of Mrs. Entwhistle's head despite her best efforts to grab them and nail them down. She began jotting down words she'd have to look up later: ISP, URL, client, web browser, upload, download, menu, screenshots, files and folders. A dull ache started in the temple beside her black eye and she rubbed it. Dex noticed.

"Sorry, I don't mean to overwhelm you. I wish I was there," he said. "I could have ads up and running in no time, even working remotely, but I need your help from that end, and it's hard when you're not computer-savvy."

Mrs. Entwhistle appreciated his tact. "I expect you think we're idiots."

"Not for a minute," Dex said. "Unless you think I'm an idiot because I don't know how to plant a garden or can peaches or, or, whatever else y'all do."

"No, honey, I know; different strokes and all. Listen, I'll find somebody local to help us. You've got too much going on to be bothered with it."

"You know what I can do, though?" Dex said. "I can

ask my editor if she'd like a feature article about the Amish Inn. If it ran in the *Post,* that'd be the best advertising in the world, and for free."

"Do you think there's a chance she'd go for it?"

"All I can do is ask. Give me some hooks."

Mrs. Entwhistle talked about how long Max had lived in the house, the remodeling efforts taken over by a team of Amish carpenters, and the Amish girl recruited to run the inn. But there she stalled.

"But, see, Anna May is, uh, taking some time out."

"Before she even starts?" Dex echoed Jimmy Jack.

"Yes, she's got some personal issues to work through. But maybe she'll be back, we just don't know yet."

"Tell me about the personal issues."

"Well, this is strictly off the record. I'd hate to betray Anna May's confidence, but the thing is, Anna May is thinking of leaving the Amish, and if she does, she may be permanently estranged from her entire family. So she ran away with a carnie and is living in a travel trailer while she tries to figure out what to do. You can't use any of this in an article, though. Not without Anna May's permission."

"Too bad. Having an Amish girl manager is a great hook. Is she pretty, by the way?"

"Dex Schofield! Lara, smack him for me. What a sexist question, and from him - young and woke and all!"

Lara laughed and obediently swatted Dex's arm.

"It would make great photos, that's all I'm saying," Dex protested. "Pretty girls always sell articles, you have to admit it, woke or not. Listen, let me do a little groundwork up here and I'll get back to you, okay?"

Chapter Sixteen

Pop went to see the bishop, and he went alone. This matter fell squarely within the male province. The bishop was the ultimate authority. It was he who married and buried, who preached and taught. Innovations had to go through him, and very often they stopped there.

Pop had known his bishop since they were boys together. They had both agreed at the time of their adult baptism that they would serve in church leadership roles if chosen. Pop was thankful daily that he'd not been the one chosen.

He reviewed in his mind how the process worked. Members of the Amish congregation nominated a number of men to be bishop. Then a slip of paper containing a Bible verse was inserted into a hymnal. That book was shuffled with other hymnals and each nominee drew a book. The one who got the book with the verse inside was the new leader, chosen by lot, anointed by God. Very often, the chosen one wept, and they were not happy tears.

The Amish moral code valued humility and meekness, so to be a model for how others should live was abhorrent. Plus, it was a hard and thankless job. In addition to making a living by farming or factory work, a bishop received no pay, no education, and no on-the-job training for his extra job. He taught himself to deliver sermons with only his own personal reading and interpretation of the Bible. Divine intervention was supposed to provide the necessary insight.

Once chosen, a bishop served for the rest of his life. There was no question of refusing. Pop remembered how his friend's hands shook, how his face paled when he drew the lot. The burden of his responsibilities set the Bishop apart. Now, as Pop drove his buggy to his old friend's farm, he was arriving as a congregant, not an old friend.

Bishop Yoder was in the barn cleaning stalls. He stopped when he saw he had a visitor, wiped his forehead with his bandana handkerchief and indicated a seat on nearby bales of straw. The men exchanged a few words of small talk, but both knew what they were there to discuss. They spoke in Pennsylvania Dutch.

"Yah, Joseph, I thought you'd be coming pretty quick," Bishop Yoder said.

"You know Anna May is gone," Pop said. "We let her go visit a distant relative and now she don't want to come back. She says she's going high." His voice was tight with the pain of that confession.

Bishop Yoder nodded. "I heard. You went to get her and bring her home, didn't you?"

"We did. Levi took us. I told Anna May to get ready to come home with us, and at first she obeyed me, but then a young man on a motorcycle came and took her away. It happened so fast, we didn't hardly know what hit us, and now we don't know where she is. She wrote one letter saying she was safe; that's all we know."

The Bishop looked through the dancing dust motes into the sunshine slanting through the barn door. "Ach, I'm sorry. I know it's hard."

"We don't know what to do," Pop said. "What should we do?"

"It's up to Anna May now," the Bishop said. "You know how it works: if she wants to return to Amish ways, she can. She hasn't joined church yet, so she would confess her sins and ask for forgiveness. Everyone would welcome her back."

"What about the miting?" Pop asked. "Would it apply to Anna May?"

"No. Because she's not a baptized member of the church, you wouldn't have to shun her. However, you have younger children. You would want to take care that they aren't influenced by a big sister who has chosen worldly ways. Also, other Amish might feel it was their duty to shame her."

Pop sighed. "Is there anything I can do to heal this situation?"

"We've all known her since she was a baby, and as a church, we would grieve her loss. But I believe what the Bible tells us in Second Corinthians: 'Be ye not unequally yoked together with unbelievers: for what fellowship hath righteousness with unrighteousness? and what communion hath light with darkness?'"

Pop bowed his head in submission, but his heart ached as he drove the buggy down the long lane to the road. He knew he was overdue for a difficult conversation with Mom, and now that he had the guidance of the Bishop, it could be put off no longer. He expected either an angry outburst or a flood of tears at the thought of losing their eldest daughter.

But she surprised him.

"I figured," she said, dry-eyed and composed. "We know families that have lost young ones to the English. It turns the whole household upside down. Now we have to go through the same thing with Anna May. She's a headstrong girl who has made some real bad choices, and she'll have to live with them. I'm sad and sorry, but I've got other children to raise. I won't have her coming and going, making the little ones think it's all right, the way she's acting. If she chooses to go high, I won't see her again."

She set her chin and Pop knew there would be no more words from her. Part of him was relieved that he didn't have to deal with a sobbing woman, but another part was amazed at her detachment. He didn't feel it himself. What he felt was a heavy lump where he imagined his heart to be.

~*~

Mrs. Entwhistle and Maxine huddled before Maxine's laptop like pioneers around a campfire. They'd managed to get through to a live person on the Help Desk, but clearly that person lived in a land far away.

"I'm sorry, I didn't understand that," Maxine said for the dozenth time. "Could you please talk more slowly? I'm so sorry, I'm sure you speak English very well, it's just hard for me to understand you over the phone."

"Please to check the CPU. If your hard disc is reaching capacity, you will have to delete files no longer needed."

Maxine and Mrs. Entwhistle made big eyes at each other. "What's a CPU, please?" Maxine asked timidly.

There was a silence they could only interpret as incredulous.

"Uh, central processing unit."

"Oh, sure, okay."

They shook their heads. "Where is it?" Mrs. Entwhistle hissed.

Maxine threw up her hands.

"Please to go to Device Manager to make sure there are no driver issues," said the sing-song voice from the other side of the world.

"Um, where would I find that?" Maxine asked in a very small voice.

Again, that pregnant pause. "Perhaps you could just reboot your computer," the voice said.

"You mean turn it off and then back on?" Maxine did know how to do that.

So, they turned the computer off and then back on again and again. Their helper seemed to be working from a list written in an arcane language they didn't understand. When he reached the end, he simply went back to Step One. They had rebooted the computer so many times, Mrs. Entwhistle thought the poor machine must have a severely sore posterior. She heard desperation creeping into the voice at the other end of the line. Maxine mimed pulling out her hair.

"We might as well give up, we're not getting anywhere," Mrs. Entwhistle whispered. "Just hang up."

But Maxine shook her head. She was incapable of ending the call on a bad note. "Say, I'm just wondering," she said pleasantly, "where are you located?"

"Bangalore, India, madam," came a reluctant response. "But I am fully trained to help you."

"And I'm sure you're doing a fine job; we're just not very savvy on this end. My goodness, you are far away! Do you have a wife and family?"

There was a pause. "I recently married. My wife and

I just learned we are expecting our first child." He sounded more like a human and less like a robot now.

"Well, isn't that wonderful! Congratulations, honey. Is she feeling well, your wife?"

"Y-y-es, I think she is well."

"You tell her we said hi all the way from America." Maxine said. "You've been so patient with us. Thank you for trying to help, and I'm sorry we're such poor students. Good luck with the new baby."

"Wasn't he nice," Maxine said after the connection was broken. "It must be hard on the poor man, trying to work with people from so far away, and English isn't even his native language, plus we're not too bright about tech."

Mrs. Entwhistle felt wrung out, even though all she'd been doing was sitting and staring at a screen. "I reckon we're no dumber than most he talks to. If people knew what they were doing, they wouldn't need tech support."

"Do you suppose a lot of folks are frustrated when they call and take it out on him? I hope his feelings weren't hurt when I couldn't understand him."

"Well, Max, you could charm the horns off a billy goat. Don't be too worried about his feelings."

Maxine stood and took a couple of stiff steps. "Ouch, I sat too long," she said."Let me get us some tea."

She knew Mrs. Entwhistle's kitchen as well as she knew her own, and soon produced the tea and one chocolate chip cookie. "It's all you have left," she said.

"Let's split it," Mrs. Entwhistle said.

"What we need is a young person," Maxine said, taking the last bite of her half of the cookie. "Ronnie Sue could probably help, but she's so busy with the beauty shop these days."

"And Dex has too much going on. I don't have the heart to bother him again."

The sounds of children returning home from school reached them. Mrs. Entwhistle cocked her head to one side and held up a finger. She rose and went to the door.

"Allen!" she called. "Allen, could you come here a minute?"

Allen lived two doors down, and at twelve had turned from grubby cherub into cool dude. She saw him hitch up his low-riding pants, and noticed he was sprouting peach fuzz on his upper lip. She grieved for his formerly pinchable cheeks, but everything changes, she reminded herself.

"Yo, Mrs. E., 'sup?" Allen slouched like his favorite rapper.

"We need your giant brain," Mrs. Entwhistle said, beckoning him into the house.

Allen pulled a chair up to the computer, tapping keys while asking a few questions and importing some photos from Maxine's phone.

"There you go," he said, after an impossibly short time. "You've got a website and some Facebook ads. People can follow the link to the website and reserve from there. Easy peasy."

He left happily clutching a ten-dollar bill in one hand and his saggy pants in the other.

"He didn't even break a sweat," Maxine marveled.

"Youth is wasted on the young," Mrs. Entwhistle said.

They didn't know enough to ask if the ads were live.

Sleep eluded Levi. He couldn't get Anna May off his mind. The thought of losing his favorite sister, the one closest to him in age, struck him as ridiculous, but he couldn't figure out what to do about it. Even if he refused to shut her out, he feared his soon-to-be wife would insist upon it. Adah was old-school in her view of the world, and she was scrupulous about rule following. Her family always participated in publicly shaming and scolding other Amish who had transgressed. It was a way of maintaining discipline, but Levi had always hated it. He felt an unwelcome niggle of doubt about his upcoming marriage. An Amish man was widely thought to rule the household, but he knew better. If he was going to do anything to help his sister, he'd have to do it before he married.

He searched for a course of action, but he didn't even know where Anna May was living. Finding her would be step one. And when he did, he'd...there his thoughts stopped. He didn't know what he'd do. Anna May was an adult and a strong one. She would have her own ideas about how to proceed with her life, and he had a feeling she wouldn't take kindly to interference.

Besides, what did he honestly think she should do? Come home, resume her Amish life even though it wasn't what she wanted? Resign herself to years of frustration and discontent? Or cut herself off from her family and support system, cast herself into the wide world and try to survive? Neither option seemed promising.

Levi hoped he'd have some kind of instinctual flash of knowledge when he faced Anna May. Because he knew he had to face her. He had to at least try to heal the rift in his family. With that much resolved, he turned over and finally slept.

In the morning, he waited until he and Pop were finished with the chores and were back in the house having a second cup of coffee. Mom was out in the yard, hanging billowing clothes on the long lines with the younger children clustered around, handing her clothespins. He and Pop were alone in the house.

"Pop, I want to find Anna May and have a talk with her," Levi said.

Pop nodded, but said nothing.

"It's just that I don't want to lose her," Levi continued, watching his father carefully. "It don't seem right; it don't seem like a loving God would want that."

"We don't question the bishop's guidance," his father said woodenly, "or your Mom's. If Anna May leaves the Amish, she won't be welcome here at home."

"Did Mom say that?"

"She did."

Levi shook his head as if to get water out of his ears. "Well, I don't agree, but it's your call. At least I want to know for myself that Anna May is safe and doing what she wants to do. Will you give me your blessing to go and find her?"

"Yah," Pop said, and Levi didn't miss the brightening of his father's face. "I would do it if I could. You're not baptized yet, not a member of the church, so you have more freedom to do...what you think is right. Maybe she'll listen to you if you tell her to come home."

"Then I'll leave today. I'll find her, Pop, and I'll do my best to make sure she's okay, but I can't promise she'll come home."

Levi threw a couple of changes of his English rumspringa clothes into a duffel bag and set out walking. His car had long been a denizen of the scrap yard, and he couldn't afford to rent a car. He'd have to hire a driver. Amish often hired their English friends to take them places a horse and buggy couldn't reach, but Levi knew he couldn't ask any of the regular drivers to take him on this journey. It was too far, for one thing. More importantly, he needed someone who wasn't too curious, was game for just about anything, and wouldn't feed the gossip mill back home. Fortunately, he had just such a friend.

Abraham Miller was still on rumspringa. He worked in a trailer factory making good money, which he spent as rapidly as possible every weekend. Levi walked the four miles to the dilapidated farm house where Abe lived with three other Amish boys. He knew Abe would be home from work by two p.m., having started his shift at six. Levi kicked aside the beer cans littering the porch, sat down and waited.

When Abe rumbled up in his Dodge Challenger, he was already drinking beer. A clattering avalanche of cans preceded him when he opened his door. Levi sighed. This was going to be a challenging trip in more ways than one.

But Abe was up for it. Once Levi had explained what he wanted, Abe grabbed a trash bag, threw a few things in it and declared himself ready to roll. Levi took the precaution of removing the six-packs from the back seat, and they were off. Taking no breaks and ignoring speed limits, they reached Mrs. Entwhistle's house at two in the morning. Abe insisted on cruising Main Street first, looking for what he called the night life. When it became painfully apparent there wasn't any, he parked in Mrs. Entwhistle's driveway, curled up in the back seat and fell instantly asleep. Levi stretched out his legs in the front seat, laid his head back and slept, too.

They were awakened by sharp rapping on the

window.

"Levi? Is that you? Wake up!" Mrs. Entwhistle cupped her hands on the foggy glass and peered into the car.

Levi's first glimpse of the new day was Mrs. Entwhistle's worried face inches from his own. He hoped she didn't see him jump.

"Yah, it's me," he said, lowering the window. "Hope we didn't scare you. I'm looking for Anna May."

"You'd better come in," Mrs. Entwhistle said. She gave a little shriek when another figure rose from the back seat. "Oh! I didn't know there was someone with you."

"This is Abe," Levi said. "He drove me."

"Well, both of you come on in and get some breakfast."

Fortified by coffee, bacon and eggs, the young men rebounded from their tough night as only the young can do. Levi set forth his mission.

"Our family needs to know that Anna May is okay. We want to give her another chance to come home if she wants to. Mom and Pop can't go looking for her, so it's up to me."

"I've seen her recently," Mrs. Entwhistle said. "She told me she was fine, that she was working out some things in her mind and needed to be away from everyone while she did it. I know the boy she's living with, Joey. He's not a bad sort, just a rolling stone. I think he's good to Anna May, but I also think he'd forget her in ten minutes if she wasn't there."

"But he came after her. That was him, the guy on the bike who took her away, right?"

"Yes, that's true. Maybe his feelings run deeper than I think. In any case, it's Anna May's feelings we're concerned about. I know she doesn't want to be found, but I don't agree with her about that. In my opinion, it's perfectly reasonable that she talks through any decision she makes with her family. Down the road, she'll be glad she did. I think I can help you locate her."

Mrs. Entwhistle went to her computer and pulled up the website for Mid-American Amusements. The schedule gave their location in a town two counties over. "It's a bit of a drive. I expect you're tired after driving all night," she said.

"Not a problem," Abe assured her. "We're up for it, right, Levi?"

"I think we can make it," Levi said, laughing.

Mrs. Entwhistle shrugged. "All right, then," she said. "I'll get my purse."

"You're coming with us?" Abe asked in astonishment.

"Of course. Anna May might need some moral support from another female."

Abe insisted that Mrs. Entwhistle ride shotgun, as he called it, and so she was ensconced in the front seat beside him with Levi in the back. Mrs. Entwhistle told Maxine later that she'd never had such a ride in her life, including the Tilt-A-Whirl at the fair. She blessed the inventor of the seat belt over and over as she braced herself on the dashboard with both hands.

"I don't believe in pestering God with pleas for deliverance from a situation I've put myself in," she said as she emerged from the car on rubbery legs. "But I'll admit I said a few prayers on this trip."

Abe laughed and gave her a friendly pat on the shoulder. "You're a trooper, Mrs. E. Do you want to drive on the way back?"

"Well, I just might," she said, adjusting her clothing and patting her hair. "I just might."

Chapter Seventeen

Anna May lifted her head from the toilet bowl and pushed her hair from her face. The pain in her belly was relentless, and now she was vomiting. Too tired and dizzy to make the trek back to bed, she lay on the bathroom floor.

That was how they found her, Mrs. Entwhistle, Levi and Abe. When no one answered their knocks, they called her name. Still no answer. Levi turned the knob and the door swung open. Glancing at each other, they entered the trailer as warily as cats in a strange place.

"Anna May?" Mrs. Entwhistle called.

Her naturally loud voice reverberated throughout the tiny space. The only answer was a low moan. Their heads swiveled, searching for the source.

"Back there," Levi said, leading the way down the narrow hallway to the bathroom. "Ammay! You're sick. Can you get up?"

Mrs. Entwhistle elbowed him aside and knelt, her hand on Anna May's forehead. "You've got a fever," she said calmly. "And it seems you've been sick to your stomach. Anything else?"

"Oh, my stomach," Anna May moaned.

"Where?"

"Here." She indicated a spot on her lower right side.

"Ah." Mrs. Entwhistle stood, crowding the boys back into the hall. "She needs to be seen by a doctor. I want to take her to Dr. Patel. Levi, grab a pillow and a couple of towels. Abe, pull the car up as close to the door as you can. Anna May, honey, you just sit there for a minute until I come get you."

Mrs. Entwhistle went into the kitchen area, sat at the table and pulled a notebook and pen from her purse.

Joey, she wrote, *Anna May is sick. I've taken her home with me to see a doctor.*

She signed her name, added her phone number, and pinned the note down with a salt shaker. Then she went back to the bathroom. Anna May had managed to sit upright, but she was shivering.

Mrs. Entwhistle stepped into the adjoining bedroom and grabbed the blanket from the bed. She wrapped it around Anna May's shaking shoulders and supported her as she led her to the car.

"I've got you now," she said quietly. "You're going to be all right."

The trip home was less of a carnival ride, but still undertaken at great speed. Mrs. Entwhistle willed the car to go even faster. Sitting in the back with Anna May's head in her lap, she stroked the damp hair from the girl's burning face.

She was alarmed at Anna May's condition, but what she projected was calmness and certainty. No point in adding to Anna May's fear with her own concerns.

"Don't go to my house," she instructed Abe as they neared town. "We're going straight to Dr. Patel's office on Main Street." She pulled out her phone and called to let the office know they were coming.

Dr. Patel emerged from the back door as they pulled into his parking lot. He took Mrs. Entwhistle's place in the back seat, where he did a quick examination of his new patient.

"Go to the hospital," he said when he emerged. "I'll meet you there."

Anna May was loaded onto a stretcher at the emergency department door and that was the last they saw of her for an hour.

Mrs. Entwhistle called Maxine from the waiting room, and she came at once. Levi and Abe paced. The women sat quietly. In their long lives, they'd had much experience with watching and waiting. They knew how to do it.

Dr. Patel appeared suddenly, starched white coat flapping behind him. He beckoned them into a small family room and into chairs.

"Anna May has appendicitis," he said abruptly. "She needs to have an operation immediately. Her appendix is ready to burst with infection, and I don't want that to happen. This hospital has one general surgeon, and he is operating on another patient right now, so I shall do the procedure myself." He turned to the boys. "Are either of you relatives?"

"I'm her brother," Levi said. His face was white, but his voice was steady.

"I'll ask you to sign the consent form. Anna May is barely conscious and can't make an informed consent. Please see the intake nurse. Now I must take care of my patient."

Maxine and Mrs. Entwhistle exchanged glances. They knew Dr. Patel was most cryptic when he was doing his best doctoring, but Levi and Abe looked shell-shocked.

"Is he any good?" Levi asked. "He sure seems... abrupt."

"It's just his way, honey," Maxine said. "He's a wonderful doctor; you have to overlook his bedside manner. He may fall a little short on people skills, but believe me, medically Anna May couldn't be in better hands."

They waited. Levi and Abe made repeated trips to the vending machine for snacks they didn't eat. Mrs. Entwhistle and Maxine sat quietly, conserving their energy. Eventually, Sanjay Patel returned, his features drawn with weariness.

"She's okay," he said, waving his hand as if to erase

the anxiety on their faces. "It was a tough surgery. The appendix was leaking, and I had some extensive clean-up to do in her abdomen. I'm going to keep her here for a couple of days to make sure there's no infection. She's in the recovery room right now, and once she's stable, I'd prefer she go straight to her room with no visitors. She's not up to it. You can all go home now."

Without waiting for questions, exclamations or thanks, Dr. Patel pivoted and disappeared behind a door that firmly said, "No Admittance." The waiting group shook their heads and looked at each other.

"So, I guess she's okay?" Levi said. "Is that what he said?"

Mrs. Entwhistle nodded. "I *think* so."

"She had a worse-than-usual bout of appendicitis; now that the operation's over, she needs quiet and rest to recover," Maxine interpreted. "He'll keep a close watch over her. Dr. Patel is extremely conscientious."

Levi nodded. "I sure wish my folks were here. This is scary stuff."

"Well, come on back to my house," Mrs. Entwhistle said. "You can stay the night. Maybe she'll be up to visitors tomorrow."

Her mind produced a hasty list of things needed to put up two more people. Clean sheets, towels, groceries. Dinner! She'd have to...Her thoughts were interrupted by Abe talking to Levi.

"Buddy, I can't stay. I've gotta work on Monday. Do you want me to leave you here?"

"I can't stay, either," Levi said. "I'm getting married. Looks like I'm not going to have a chance to talk to Anna May after all. It was a wasted trip."

"No, it wasn't," Mrs. Entwhistle said. "What would have happened if you hadn't come looking for her? You showed up when she really needed you. You go on home with your mind at ease; tell your parents Anna May is getting excellent care. When you're ready to come back, bring your new wife. You're both always welcome."

~*~

Mrs. Entwhistle heard the *ping* of her computer that signaled an incoming message. She opened one eye and glanced at the bedside clock. 3:23, it said in huge neon letters. Mrs. Entwhistle didn't need her glasses for that clock.

Must be Spam. No civilized person would e-mail at this hour. If it was about Anna May, someone would call me on the telephone.

She noticed that Roger hadn't reacted at all, not to the *ping* and not to her sudden stirring. Poor old Rog. His deafness was both a blessing and a curse. He was bothered by very little these days, but he also missed things over which he used to enjoy creating a commotion. Mrs. Entwhistle thought wistfully of Roger's puppy days. He'd been a lively little fellow, zooming around the house and then abruptly falling into a puddle of deep sleep. She missed that dog, but she was not as lively as she used to be, either, yet she still enjoyed life. She thought Roger did, too. With that, she turned over and went back to sleep.

In the morning, she checked her computer. There was a reservation request for the Amish Inn.

"The first one!" she told Roger. "The ads must be running already. But I wonder why I got it? I guess because that's how Allen set it up. We never thought to tell him to give the Inn's email address. Oh, boy, wait until I tell Maxine!"

But Maxine was horrified. "Oh, no! A reservation? The Inn's not even open. I don't have anyone to run the place. When do they want to come? How many of them are there? I'm not ready."

"Let's see. It's a Mr. and Mrs. Devon, just one couple, looks like. They want to come on December 24, Christmas Eve. Hmmm, makes a person wonder why they wouldn't be home with their family."

"Christmas Eve!" Maxine was actually wringing her hands. Mrs. Entwhistle stopped to register that she'd never seen anyone wring their hands before. "Christmas Eve, and we aren't decorated; there's not so much as a sprig of holly in that house. I suppose they read Dex's piece in the *Post* or saw the Facebook ads and went to the website like Allan said they would. What did he put on there, anyway?"

Mrs. Entwhistle pulled up the site, and sure enough, it said the Inn was open for business. "We should have read the copy more carefully," she said. "We were so happy to check that chore off our To Do list, we got careless."

"Haste makes waste," Maxine said mournfully. "Well, I'll have to get in touch with the Devons and tell them there's been a mistake. Maybe they'd like to come later. I could offer a discount."

"Now, wait, Max. Let's think a minute before you tell them no. You'd originally planned a soft opening the first of December and then opening for real the week of Christmas, right?"

"Right. But with Anna May so sick and nobody to run the place, I mentally moved the Inn's opening to springtime. I never thought to change the website. I guess people can't read my mind."

"How about this: we'll get Allen to revise the ads and the website, but let the Devons come. With just one couple staying, it will give you a chance to trouble-shoot without pressure. Anna May is out of commission, but there's you and me, and Anjali said she'd help."

"I know, but I hate to ask her."

"She'd love it, and Shyam would, too. They miss their Patel Paradise Motel days. They'll be like two old war horses called into battle. The Devons can be your practice guests."

"I don't know." Maxine's doubt was written all over her face, but she agreed to at least ask the Patels.

"We would be delighted," Anjali said. "We can still observe the holiday with Sanjay and Delilah and JJ, since their home is nearby. We are honored to be the ones to help open your wonderful new inn."

The Patels flexed their innkeeper muscles convincingly, and Maxine followed their expert lead. She confirmed with the Devons that they were expected on December 24 for their proposed two-night stay, making sure they knew the town would be closed down for Christmas day, but the Inn would serve extra meals to compensate. Maxine's heart was jumping as she pressed Send. Her first guests!

The Inn would soon be launched, albeit very quietly, and that was exciting. But it was only the beginning. Presumably, more guests would arrive and have to be fed and watered and put to bed. The Patels couldn't be her innkeepers forever. Maxine was a knot of anxiety.

"Maybe I've made an awful mistake," she said to Mrs. Entwhistle. "Maybe it was a stupid idea to spend so much money on making my old house into an inn."

Mrs. Entwhistle made soothing sounds and patted Maxine down as best she could, all the while jiggling a thought around in her head, one she didn't share with her friend. Best to do a little leg-work before mentioning it. Maxine had enough on her mind.

Anna May did not have health insurance, and she was frantic about the costs her operation and hospital stay were incurring. Mrs. Entwhistle and Dr. Patel stood at her bedside and listened.

"When Amish families have medical bills, the church

pays from a fund we all contribute to," Anna May said through tears. "But I'm not in good standing with the church, and I don't know how I'll be able to pay. I've got to get out of here before I run up more bills."

"You won't get a bill from me," Dr. Patel said. "As for the hospital, it's a not-for-profit facility and is legally required to offer indigent care. I'll send a rep from the billing office to help you fill out the paperwork. I understand your wish to leave before incurring more expense; however, I want you to receive IV antibiotics for another couple of days to be sure there is no residual infection." He stopped and thought for a moment. "Excuse me; let me check on something."

He stepped into the hall, and Anna May and Mrs. Entwhistle could hear him talking quietly on his phone. When he returned, he was smiling.

"I'd like to invite Anna May to stay with my wife and me for a couple of days," he said. "Delilah and I can monitor her as carefully as the hospital would, and I'll administer the IV antibiotics myself. If that's okay with you, Anna May?"

"Oh, I couldn't impose on you and Delilah like that," Anna May said, her eyes brimming with tears.

Dr. Patel waved away her objection. "You're a friend," he repeated. "Delilah insists you come to us, and I never argue with her. Happy wife, happy life." Sanjay Patel grinned like the blissfully happy newly-wed he was.

~*~

Anna May's recovery was true to Dr. Patel's prognosis. She spent a couple of days and nights at the Patels' home, sleeping deeply, eating Delilah's cooking and playing gentle games with JJ, who had been cautioned to use his indoor voice and gentlest manners.

"But it's time for me to go," Anna May said to Delilah on the morning of the third day. "I've got to make some plans for my future."

"What do *you* want to do?" Delilah asked, mopping up the table where JJ had recently spilled his milk. "Do you want to go home to your parents and the Amish way of life?"

"That's the only thing I know for sure," Anna May responded. "I felt so confused when I was sort of hiding out with Joey. Somehow, being so sick and having an operation made me think more clearly. I don't want to go home again. Part of me is sad about causing my parents such grief, but I know I can't return, not and be true to myself. So now I have to figure out what I do next, how I'll support myself and where I'll live."

"Don't you have a job running the Amish Inn?"

"I did. But I can't expect Maxine to hire me now that I've proved to be so undependable."

Delilah smiled. "I think you should ask her before you make any decisions. You may be pleasantly surprised. That is, if you're still interested in the job."

"Of course, I am," Anna May said. "It would be perfect for me right now. This winter while the guests are sparse, I could start studying for my GED. That's the first step to going on to college."

"Ah! I can help you there," Delilah said. "I've gone down that same path myself. When I came here with JJ, I was an unmarried teenage mother with a very new GED, and I only got that because my aunt helped me."

"Really? But now you're the wife of the town doctor and almost a lawyer." Anna May shook her head in wonder.

"True. It happened fast, but none of it would have happened at all if I hadn't had help, and a lot of it came from Mrs. Entwhistle and Maxine. They're ready to help you, too, and so am I. Mrs. Entwhistle said something to me once that I've always remembered. She said when you want something, you take a step toward it. One step leads to another, and all kinds of unexpected things happen from forward momentum. You can't see it when you start, but you summon all your courage and take that first step. Believe me, you can do it."

Anna May's eyes suddenly filled with tears. "You're all so good to me," she said brokenly.

"And you're exhausted," Delilah said. "Now off you go to have a nap. We have all the time in the world to figure out that next step."

Chapter Eighteen

Levi was having an intense conversation with his parents. He'd filled them in on Anna May's illness, operation and recovery. Levi knew his Mom would go to her bedroom and cry when they were finished talking, but for now, she was made of steel.

"Does Anna May want to come home to recover?" she asked.

"I don't think so, Mom," Levi said gently.

"Well, what about her hospital bills? How does she think she's going to pay them without help?"

"The town doc, the guy who did the operation, took care of all that. He invited her to his house to finish recuperating. It's okay; he has a family and everything," he said quickly as looks of alarm spread across his parents' faces. "He's a friend of Mrs. Entwhistle's."

"Ach, that woman! She's the one who started this whole mess," Mom said.

"Now that ain't exactly fair," Pop said. "Anna May asked to go visit her; all Mrs. Entwhistle did was agree. I'd say Anna May is making her own decisions, and we should be grateful to Mrs. Entwhistle for helping her."

"Yah, helping her leave home and go high," Mom said bitterly. "I know I'm supposed to forgive that woman, but it's going to take a while."

"Mrs. Entwhistle ain't like that, Mom," Levi protested. "She's been real good to Anna May, and to Abe and me when we were there. She says she wants Anna May to make up her own mind, and she won't do anything to influence her one way or another."

"Well, she should stick to stuff she knows something about," Mom muttered, turning away.

Levi knew it was easier to be mad than sad, and that his mother was handling her grief by hiding it behind anger. They were not a demonstrative family, but he reached out and took her hand. She tightened her grip for a second before getting up to pour more coffee, but her face softened a little.

"What can't be cured must be endured," she said. "You tell Anna May that if she leaves the Amish, she leaves her family. She won't be welcome here. You tell her that, Levi, and make sure she understands."

Levi and his father exchanged glances. The matriarch of the family had spoken.

~*~

Mrs. Entwhistle wasn't especially good at keeping secrets. She usually told Maxine everything as a matter of course. It was hard to not mention what her mind was full of these days. She concentrated on all the holiday things that had to be done: decorating, baking, entertaining, shopping and wrapping. Never mind Christmas cards, she'd skip them this year.

Her town was too far south to provide ice skating or skiing, and instead often brought forth sunny days with temperatures in the 70's. Everyone spoke longingly of a white Christmas, but in Mrs. Entwhistle's memory that had only happened twice, and the snow was gone almost as soon as it hit the warm earth.

This year was especially busy because of all the extra plans for the Inn. The Devons were expected on December 24th and Maxine was in a frenzy of preparation. Anna May was finished with her IV therapy and would soon leave the Patels' home. Where she would go next was the most pressing issue.

"I can't come back and stay with you indefinitely," she wailed to Mrs. Entwhistle on the phone. "It's not fair on you. I don't even have a job so I could pay you rent."

"What's all this talk about paying?" Mrs. Entwhistle said. "I won't have it, you know. You are my friend and my relative; you are always welcome in my home."

"And I appreciate it more than I can say, but I must DO something."

"Of course, you want to take control of your own life. Let's think what a first step might be."

"I need a job so I can pay for a place to live."

"Don't you already have a job and a place to live, running the Inn?"

"I don't think so. I can't expect Maxine to trust me when I ran off and left her hanging."

Mrs. Entwhistle asked, "Have you apologized to her?"

"No. I'm ashamed to face her."

"That won't do," Mrs. Entwhistle said gently. "Whether you continue with the Inn or not, you owe Max a sincere apology. Do it for yourself to remove the guilt you are carrying. You're eating your heart out about it, aren't you?"

Anna May nodded, then realized Mrs. Entwhistle couldn't see her. There was a long silence on the line.

"Well, you think about it, honey," Mrs. Entwhistle said.

Anna May did. Then she punched in Maxine's number.

"There's something I need to say to you in person," Anna May said. "I'd come to you if I could."

"I'll drop by, honey." Maxine had been expecting a call like this. "We need to talk."

~*~

Looking into Maxine's kind eyes, Anna May spoke from her heart. "I'm so sorry I ran off and left you after you'd been so kind to me. You offered me the job of running the Inn and I really wanted to do that. Then when my parents showed up, it just seemed like everything went out of my head. I felt like a naughty little girl again, told to go out and cut the switch that would be used on me. Joey just...No, I won't blame him. I need to own all my decisions. I don't expect you to hire me now, and I completely understand. I just wanted to say how sorry I am and to ask your forgiveness."

Maxine was silent for a moment. Then she said, "What you did was stressful for me. I was left in a quandary about the inn—whether to try to run it myself, find somebody else, or just scrap the whole idea. I'd already moved into my new house, so my bridges were pretty well burned. And of course, I was worried about you and your well-being. It was an extra burden. I'm not saying this to make you feel worse, but I think it's important that we both be honest."

Anna May nodded. For a moment, neither of them spoke.

"I understand," Anna May said. "I don't deserve to be forgiven."

Maxine smiled and reached for Anna May's hand. "But of course I forgive you, child. You're young and trying to figure out your new world. Every one of us makes mistakes, especially when we're getting started as adults. I appreciate your apology and I accept it. The job offer still stands if you want it."

Anna May's face lit up. "Really? You'd still hire me?"

"Well, sure. You're perfect for the job, and the job is perfect for you. I think you learned a lot from your experiences. That's all any of us can hope for, right?"

"So, when can I start?"

"As soon as Dr. Patel says you're ready. In the meantime, you're welcome to move into your room at the Inn. You can rest and regain your strength while you're learning to feel at home."

Marcie and Chad Devon had different packing styles. Marcie wrapped her garments in tissue paper and rolled them carefully. Chad grabbed things from hangers and drawers and slung them into his suitcase. Marcie knew Chad would look like a Ralph Lauren ad in his clothes, and she'd look like a What Not to Wear example. It was so unfair.

This trip was probably a bad idea. They'd found themselves with no plans for the holidays after both sets of parents opted for island trips. Neither Marcie nor Chad had siblings ("which means we didn't learn to share," Marcie said meaningfully), so unless they, too, wanted a tropical Christmas, they were on their own.

"Let's go island-hopping, then," Chad said, always up

for adventure.

But Marcie said no. "I have to be at work on December 26th. We've got that big case coming up and it's all hands on deck. I'm lucky to have Christmas Eve and Day off."

Both were downcast at the thought of the two of them trying to be jolly in their tiny city apartment. The days were long gone when just being together was enough.

Being in constant motion allowed them to delay the difficult conversation they both knew they'd have to have eventually. While they couldn't travel far, travel they must.

It was Marcie who saw the feature article in the Washington Post. "Mom used to live in this tiny little town. She was always talking about the slow pace, the nice people, the easy life. I think I'd like to spend a couple of days there and just chill. Doesn't that sound good?"

"Sounds boring," Chad said briefly.

"Well, you come up with something, then."

"I did. Island-hopping, remember? You said no."

"And you know why I said no."

They glared at each other. Marcie stalked to her computer. She wielded the mouse balefully before she returned to Chad. "I've booked us at someplace called the Amish Inn for Christmas Eve and Christmas Day. It's some kind of bed and breakfast in Mom's home town. Looks nice online."

"What is there to do there?" Chad asked.

"Probably nothing."

"Really? Nothing?"

"Nope."

They looked at each in dismay. "Why are we going, then?" Chad asked.

Marcie had no answer. Choosing the Inn had been an impulsive slap at Chad, and now it seemed like a very bad idea.

~*~

Mrs. Entwhistle and Anjali Patel were deep in conspiracy. It was hard to find a way to communicate without Maxine joining them.

"This must be how people who have affairs feel," Mrs. Entwhistle said. "Sneaking around, making covert plans. It *is* kind of exciting."

"Yes, and we do not have to buy uncomfortable underwear," Anjali said, laughing.

"What is this about underwear?" Shyam asked from the door as he entered.

"Never mind, it is just a little women's joke," Anjali said.

"But not a bad conversational topic," Shyam replied with a grin.

"Shyam! You will make me blush in front of our friend!"

"Is everything ready at the Inn, do you think?" Mrs.

Entwhistle said, getting back to business. "Do you need anything else bought or picked up or done?"

"No, I think not. Now we need to get Anna May settled in the main floor bedroom, and then she will have several days to rest before the arrival of our first guests."

"It seems too much to ask you to prepare so much food, though," Mrs. Entwhistle said. "It's just supposed to be a bed and *breakfast*, not lunch and dinner as well."

"It is just this once, when all the restaurants in town are closed for the holiday. You and I will make some Indian dishes we know everyone will like. It will be fun. And Shyam will see that the fire in the living room is burning, the special surprise is installed, and the wine is ready to pour."

"I figured out how to keep Maxine away until we're ready. I arranged for her daughter in Australia to call at just the right time and keep her mother on the phone for an hour. Lord knows what the phone bill will be, but Geraldine thinks it's great fun to be part of the surprise. Max will be on pins and needles to get off the phone and over to the Inn, but she'd never dream of cutting Geraldine short."

"There are so many secrets!" Anjali said happily. "Anna May knows some of them, Maxine knows some of them, but neither knows all of them. It reminds me of holidays back in India, when we would prepare surprises for each family member. I remember one year mine was a trip to Agra to see the Taj Mahal. It was my engagement present from

Shyam. He said it was good luck to visit a monument to true love as we planned our wedding."

"And was it?"

"Oh, yes. You see us still together and happy after all these years."

Mrs. Entwhistle's smile was wistful. Her own marriage had lasted more than half a century, but it seemed to her it had passed in a blink. She wondered what Floyd would think if he could see her today, what he'd think of the world she now lived in. Outwardly, she supposed it looked very much the same; no one could see how much her interior landscape had shifted. With a slight shake of the head, she brought her attention back to the matters at hand.

"I'm not sure what to do about Roger," she said

"What do you mean, do about him? Roger will come to the Inn with everyone else."

"He's so old, I'm afraid he'll get tired out from all the excitement."

They both looked at Roger deeply asleep in his favorite corner of the sofa. Anjali laughed.

"I do not think you have to worry. Roger seems to be able to sleep anywhere. Bring his special pillows and we will make a quiet corner for him to retreat to when he feels overwhelmed."

"I may need such a corner myself," Mrs. Entwhistle said.

Chapter Nineteen

Christmas Eve dawned fiery red on the eastern horizon. Mrs. Entwhistle tried to remember the old couplet: "Evening red, morning gray, sends the traveler on his way. Evening gray, morning red, sends the traveler to his bed." Whatever that meant. She had too much to do to worry about the weather.

First order of business was smuggling Anna May's surprise into the Inn. Louise and Henry Hershberger had called her a month ago in high spirits.

"You'd never guess what we found!" Louise said.

"Then you'd better tell me."

"A portrait of Jonas Hershberger! It was in the attic, all wrapped up in brown paper. Apparently it's been up there for decades, and we didn't even know it. Henry and I both think it's remarkable that Jonas would have ever allowed a portrait to be painted of him. Amish don't believe in making images of themselves, so it shows how far he'd come from his roots. We think he must have had second thoughts after it was completed and just stuck it in the attic and forgot about it. The colors are as fresh and clear as the day it was painted, although, of course, it's a very muted palette, the kind they used back then. Our kids say he looks spooky because his eyes follow you, but we thought Anna May might want to see what her ancestor looked like."

Mrs. Entwhistle had listened to this recital with growing excitement. "Of course, the portrait is yours to do with whatever you choose," she said tactfully. "Do you plan to hang it in your home?"

Louise paused. "Oh, we hadn't thought that far. We *could*." She sounded less than enthusiastic. "But I don't know where we'd find room for such a large painting, and it doesn't really go with our stuff. Maybe we'll think about donating it to the local history museum."

"That's an option, certainly. Or, here's a thought. You know Maxine Gober is opening a bed and breakfast named the Amish Inn. It seems to me the portrait might find a home above the mantel there. His direct descendent and our relative, Anna May Bontrager, will be managing the Inn. It would be a nice tribute to Jonas and Anna May and their heritage."

"I remember Anna May; you brought her to the farm that time. The kids loved her. Let me talk to Henry. I'll get back to you."

Henry thought Mrs. Entwhistle's idea was super. "Nobody ever goes to the history museum, anyway," he said. "I'd rather see old Jonas up on the wall at the Amish Inn. Sounds like it could be his home away from home. Maybe we could have a plaque beside it telling about his life."

Mrs. Entwhistle shared the news with Maxine and Anjali, but she didn't tell Anna May. "Let's sneak that portrait above the mantel on Christmas Eve and let it be a surprise for her."

Jonas was at that moment leaning up against the wall in her living room, staring out of his ornate plaster frame, looking both pleased with himself and embarrassed to be there. Maxine would transport him to the Inn, and Shyam would install the portrait above the mantel when Anna May was occupied elsewhere. They all anticipated her surprise when she came upon her ancestor in pride of place in the living room.

That was the easy surprise. The others were more complicated. First on the list was getting a Christmas tree. Leaving it this late made it seem hardly worth doing, but Mrs. Entwhistle knew it was important to have a Christmas tree in the Inn this year because it would be the start of an enduring tradition. Besides, Anna May had never had one.

It was a mild day, the kind the South produces in December like a benediction. Mrs. Entwhistle got on her scooter and rode to Booger's place. She found him slumped in a rocking chair on his front porch. She dismounted and approached the house.

"Good morning, Booger," she called, seeing his head jerk up as her voice woke him.

Booger was a friend from earliest childhood, making it possible for Mrs. Entwhistle to excuse his less-savory personal habits because she knew his good heart. She smiled at him now to ease his embarrassment at being caught sleeping during the day.

"Well, Cora. What brings you here?" Booger said, wiping a hand over his furry face. Obviously, he hadn't shaved for days.

"I wondered if you might sell me a Christmas tree for the Amish Inn," Mrs. Entwhistle said.

"Don't reckon I'd sell you one, but might give you one," Booger said.

He heaved himself to his feet and gave the kind of all-over shake a dog performs after a swim. Then he made his way carefully down the steps and stood with Mrs. Entwhistle in the yard.

"We gotta go back to the tree line."

Booger climbed in the sidecar of her scooter as if he did it every day. She shrugged, got back on the scooter and started it. They puttered slowly down the long, dusty lane toward a stand of evergreens. Once there, they dismounted and walked slowly among the pines.

"That one!" Mrs. Entwhistle said. "No, that one. Wait. Maybe...That one?"

"Mebbe you oughta narrow it down some," Booger said. "How tall and how wide, that kinda thing."

"Seven feet tall and not too bushy."

"Might be a problem. Trees that tall gonna be full."

Booger walked slowly, eyeing the trees judiciously. "Now, that 'un right there. That might do if we take some off the bottom."

Mrs. Entwhistle walked around it, stumbling a little on the uneven ground.

"Now, don't you fall and break a hip, Cora," Booger cautioned her.

"Yes, I think that's the one." Mrs. Entwhistle believed she was far less likely to fall than Booger, but she didn't say anything. The man was giving her a Christmas tree, after all.

Booger whipped out his red bandana and tied it to a branch of the tree. "Caleb will cut it and bring it to you."

Caleb, Booger's long-suffering son, lived with his Deddy, as he called him, and took care of everything the old man no longer could. Mrs. Entwhistle knew Caleb would bring her a nicely-shaped tree, put it in the tree-stand, fill the pan with water and even string the lights if she wanted him to. She'd often kiddingly offered to adopt Caleb, which made him smile shyly and look down. It was a shame he was turning into an oddball like his father. Mrs. Entwhistle held out a faint hope that he'd meet a nice woman someday who'd take them both as a package deal. She couldn't imagine who that might be.

With the tree taken care of, she went back home and got on the phone. First call was to Dex. Lara answered in their Washington, D.C. home.

"Yes, we're coming. In fact, we're about to get on the road. I was just getting the baby ready," Lara said.

Baby Thomas was seven months old, an age Mrs. Entwhistle found especially endearing. He smiled most of the time, laughed heartily when amused, could sit up steadily, but hadn't mastered the art of crawling. Mrs. Entwhistle hoped that sleeping through the night in a strange place was also in his repertoire of endearing qualities.

"All right, honey, I'll see you when you get here. Remember, go straight to the Amish Inn. Park in the back after you unload so Maxine won't see your car if she drives by."

Next call was to Anjali Patel. "Dex and Lara and the baby should be here by suppertime, and the Devons are expected then, too. What should we make?"

"I think a big pot of vegetable soup and cornbread," Anjali said. "That can be served any time they arrive."

"I'll make a couple of blueberry pies for dessert," Mrs. Entwhistle said. "I froze some real good blueberries last summer. We have vanilla ice cream, right? Okay, that ought to do it for tonight. What about breakfast?"

"Maxine is baking cinnamon rolls even as we speak. I will make a huge breakfast casserole. Could you make that hot pineapple dish that is so good?"

"Of course."

Christmas lunch was fully planned with a mixture of Indian cuisine and traditional Southern dishes, and dinner that night would be left-overs. The ladies nodded their heads, satisfied that the food was under control.

"The rooms are ready. We have Dex's family in one, and the crib is made up for Thomas. Maxine and I will take the room with the two twin beds. Our paying guests have the best room that faces the street. That still leaves one empty. Are you sure you and Shyam don't want to sleep over?"

"No, we are better in our own bed. We wake very early, always, so we will be in the Inn kitchen, ready with coffee and tea when you come downstairs."

"All right then."

So that was taken care of. Maxine was expecting the Devons, her first guests. She had no idea her Inn would be full of friends on that first night, and filled with Christmas festivities all the next day. Mrs. Entwhistle would have said she was plumb worn out from all the secret planning, but truth be told, she loved it.

~*~

The ride south was a silent one for Marcie and Chad. City dwellers to the core, they didn't own a car, using ride share vehicles whenever a bus or taxi wouldn't do. The rental car they'd chosen had been unavailable at the last minute, so they'd had to settle on a far sportier model than they liked. Chad drove like a little old man, Marcie thought with irritation.

With great effort, she managed not to say anything. When it was her turn behind the wheel, she put her foot down and the little car shot forward. From the corner of her eye, she enjoyed the sight of Chad's clenched jaw and braced feet.

Finally, the hypnosis of the open road soothed them both. Marcie slowed down, and Chad speeded up. The ride became boring, just like the trips they remembered in their parents' cars when they were kids.

"What do you think it'll be like?" Marcie asked as the fence posts marched by like soldiers. "The Inn, I mean. Do you think it will be all kitschy with Amish doilies and Amish bonnets and an Amish all-you-can-eat buffet?"

"You ought to know, you booked it. What did the pictures look like?"

"Very simple, really. It looked like an old house that had been somebody's home. The rooms looked big, but sometimes online photos can be deceiving. Everything looked clean and plain," Marcie said.

"Well, even if it's a dump, we're only there for two nights. If we're really desperate, we can leave before then. What I'm wondering is what we're going to do while we're there. I mean, Christmas morning? Do we go down to breakfast, and then...What, go back to our room? Take a walk? Watch TV? Should we have brought a present for the innkeeper?"

"I don't know, Chad." Marcie's voice dripped with irritation. "I can't always plan every last detail for you. I might point out you've done nothing for this trip but pack your own clothes."

"Yeah, well, it was your big idea," Chad muttered.

Hostility rolled into the car like fog. They rode without speaking for many miles, wordlessly arriving at their destination. Chad drove slowly through the gathering dusk, listening to the GPS directions.

"Wow, talk about a one-horse town!" he said. "Actually, I doubt there's even one horse in this berg."

"But look how peaceful it is," Marcie breathed.

The streetlights came on at that moment, puddling pools of light around the wide, empty sidewalks. Lamplight shone in the houses they passed. Many windows were uncurtained and they glimpsed the twinkling of Christmas lights in living rooms and saw families gathering for supper. A couple of boys on bikes zoomed down the sidewalk, yelling at each other.

"Hurry up, the streetlights are on. We'll be in big trouble."

Chad smiled. "That was my curfew, too. When the streetlights came on, I'd better be tucked up in the family hearth."

"I never knew that," Marcie said. "I mean, I knew you grew up in a small town, but you don't talk about it much."

"It was a long time ago."

"There!" Marcie said suddenly. "Look. I think that's the Inn. Yes, there's a sign. It needs to be lighted; it's hard to read. But yes, it says Amish Inn."

They coasted gently to a stop at the curb and surveyed the old house. Every window cast forth a warm golden glow. Colored lights spangled the dusk, and a fat evergreen wreath beckoned to them from the door. Chad pulled the emergency brake on the hilly street and grabbed their overnight bags while Marcie extracted herself from the car and stretched.

As they approached the door, they were joined by another couple. Accustomed as they were to the diversity of city living, they still had to stop themselves from staring. The man was dressed in a boxy black coat, black trousers and a white shirt. On his head was a black hat, and his chin sported the wispy beginnings of a beard. The woman wore a black dress, stockings, shoes, and shawl. Her face was framed by a black bonnet that surrounded her perfectly plain, unmade-up face.

"Evening," the man said. "Looks like we're going to the same place."

"Do we just walk in, or..." Marcie's question was answered when the door was flung open.

"Come in!"

A beautiful young girl smiled warmly at them. Her face changed to a look of astonishment when she saw the Devons were not alone.

"Why, Levi! And Adah? What are you doing here? Please, come in, everyone. You're welcome, uh, to the Amish Inn."

Anna May was flustered, and she couldn't hide it. Seeing her brother and Adah—*were they married?*—had robbed her of her poise. Fortunately, Mrs. Entwhistle was close behind her.

"You must be Marcie and Chad Devon," she said, shaking their hands warmly. "We are so honored to have you as our Christmas guests. And Levi! What a nice surprise. Please, come in out of the cold. Right this way."

The Devons followed in Mrs. Enwhistle's wake, leaving Anna May staring at the couple still on the doorstep.

Levi cleared his throat and spoke. "Do you have room for a couple more?"

"Why, yes, of course, we, I mean, there is one more room left. Of course, you are welcome. Excuse me, Adah, I'm acting like such a *dumbkopf.* I'm just surprised. Are you two married now?"

"Yah," Levi said proudly. "Look, I'm growing a beard and everything. This is sort of our honeymoon."

Adah blushed and poked Levi with her sharp elbow. "You don't have to announce it to everyone," she hissed. "Besides, it's a trip, not a honeymoon."

"It's only Ammay," Levi said, rubbing his rib. "She don't care what I call it."

"When did you get married?" Anna May asked.

"Just this past Thursday," Adah said. "Then we got

on the bus and came here. I don't hardly know I'm married; it hasn't sunk in yet."

"Why did you come?" Anna May asked bluntly. "I didn't hear from anyone in the family when I had my appendix out. I thought you didn't care."

"We cared," Levi said softly, "but Mom and Pop are still sore about the way their trip to bring you home ended. They're waiting to see what you're going to do. But I told Adah before we got married, I said, Anna May will always be my sister, and she'll always be welcome in our home. I don't care what anyone else has to say about it."

"I want to start out honest, Anna May," Adah said. "I think we should shame you for your behavior. If it was up to me, we'd have nothing to do with you. But I've always obeyed my father, and now that Levi is my husband, I will obey him."

Adah, with her pinched mouth and pious ways, had always been one of the kids Anna May avoided. Her heart had sunk when Levi said he was courting her. But now they were a married couple, and, for Levi's sake, Anna May would get along with her. Somehow.

"I appreciate your honesty. I know this must be hard for you, but we're sisters now," she said. "Come into the living room, both of you. Let me take your wraps and get you something to drink. Coke? Tea?"

But Levi didn't answer. Both he and Adah were transfixed on the threshold of the big main room. It glowed with candlelight and smelled of fresh pine; a fire crackled on the hearth, and above the mantle was a large oil painting of a man who looked a bit like Levi.

"Is that...?" He pointed.

Anna May's eyes followed his finger. She gasped. She hadn't seen the portrait yet herself.

"Why, I think that's our ancestor, Jonas Hershberger. I had no idea there was a painting of him, or that it was here in the inn."

Shyam came forward smiling. "We surprised you, did we not?" he said to Anna May. "Louise and Henry found the painting in their attic and decided to hang it in the Amish Inn."

Mrs. Entwhistle descended the stairs, having seen the Devons to their room. She heard the last part of the conversation.

"Isn't it great!" she said, rubbing her hands together. "You have your relatives all around you tonight. And this must be Adah. Welcome, honey."

"Did you know they were coming?" Anna May asked accusingly.

"I did not, but Christmas surprises are the best ones of all. Levi and Adah, let me show you to your room. Luckily, we have one left, or we'd have had to put you in the manger tonight!" Her voice floated down the stairs as she escorted Levi and Adah back up the stairs she'd recently climbed down.

She's going to be exhausted, Anna May thought distractedly. In truth, she could hardly process what had just happened. The Inn was officially open and its first guests had arrived. Her brother and his new wife were among those guests, and now Jonas Hershberger's painted eyes seemed to follow her every move, not liking what they saw. The room spun, and she sat down abruptly in the nearest chair.

Shyam came forward in alarm. "Here, Anna May, just put your head down for a minute. You are very pale. Anjali! Come here, please. Quickly."

Anjali appeared wiping her hands on her apron, took one look at Anna May's face and crossed the room to her.

"You are tired, dear Anna May," she said gently. "We will help you to your room for some quiet time. Too much has happened all at once, yes? And you are still recuperating. Come, lean on Shyam's arm. Everything will be all right."

Chapter Twenty

Maxine was out of breath. "Oh, am I late? I'm so sorry! Is there anything I need to do with dinner? Geraldine called and I couldn't get off the phone. I've never known her to be so talkative! I tried to hint that I had to go, but she just went on and on. I heard more about her life in Australia in the last hour than I've heard the whole time she's been living there. Did the Devons arrive? Why is the table set for so many?"

The doorbell sounded and Maxine looked inquiringly at Mrs. Entwhistle. "Is that the Devons?"

"No, they're already here and up in their room. Who could be ringing the bell tonight?" She winked at Anjali. "Anna May is having a little rest, so why don't you answer it, Max?"

They heard Maxine's cry of delight when she opened the door. "Look, it's Dex and Lara and little Thomas!

What a wonderful surprise. Come in, come in, you're just in time for supper."

Mrs. Entwhistle was enveloped in Dex's warm hug, passed to Lara, and ended up with Thomas in her arms. The baby looked at her solemnly before reaching up to try to grab her earrings. Mrs. Entwhistle's eyes filled with tears as she saw how much Thomas looked like his Daddy. How she loved that rascal, Dex, her fellow *Pantograph* reporter, co-conspirator and partner in crime! This was going to be a very good Christmas.

"How did you ever manage to keep this a surprise?" Max asked. "Is that why the table has so many settings? And I bet you've got their room ready with the crib and everything, don't you?"

"Everything is prepared," Mrs. Entwhistle assured her. "Now, come on, Schofield family. Let's get you situated before dinner." She led the way up the stairs again, but this time she held onto the railing and walked more slowly. When she returned to the kitchen, it was to find a flushed and happy Maxine filling the wine glasses.

"I never would have believed you capable of such deviousness," Maxine said, unable to hide her smile despite her scolding tone. "To think you've known all along that Dex and Lara were coming and never breathed a word. You're a dark horse, Cora Entwhistle."

"That's not all the surprises tonight," Mrs. Entwhistle said enigmatically.

"What else?"

"Wait and see who else comes down to dinner," Mrs. Entwhistle said. "Just relax and enjoy your first night as an innkeeper. The food is ready to serve and all you have to do is sound the chimes."

Ding-dong-ding-dong.

Somewhere, Maxine had found old-fashioned dinner chimes and now she wielded the little hammer. The marimba-like sound was mellow, but it penetrated even to the upstairs rooms. One by one, bedroom doors opened and guests descended the wide stairs.

Levi and Adah came first, surprising Maxine yet again. "Levi! I can't believe my eyes! And this pretty girl must be Adah."

Introductions were made and Adah's smile was shy in the warmth of the welcome. The couple wore their somber black attire, but Adah had removed her bonnet, revealing a sheer white head covering.

Anna May emerged from her room wearing a modest dark dress, with her hair braided around her head. Mrs. Entwhistle couldn't see how anyone could find fault with such a modest appearance, but she saw Adah's mouth tighten when she looked at her sister-in-law. *Levi's got his work cut out for him with that one,* she thought.

Marcie and Chad appeared next. They'd changed from their traveling clothes and were dressed for dinner in New York. Marcie wore a severely-cut black dress with a single string of pearls. Her face look like carved ivory. Chad had on a black velvet

223

jacket. It was a little over the top for the time and place, but he knew Marcie loved it and for some reason he'd thrown it in his suitcase.

Anjali wore a deep red sari that set off her dark eyes and hair. Shyam wore a richly-brocaded dark green kurta. Together, they looked like a Christmas card, even though that tradition was very far from the ones in which they'd grown up. Mrs. Entwhistle and Maxine had chosen to wear long dresses. Mrs. Entwhistle was happy to break out her best blue dress, bought for her sixtieth high school reunion, and worn a surprising number of times since. Maxine wore purple sequins.

"Do I look too twinkly?" she asked Mrs. Entwhistle.

"Just twinkly enough."

Dex ran down the stairs carrying a baby monitor in one hand. "He's asleep," he said, "and Lara will be down in a minute. She said not to wait, for everyone to be seated and begin. She'll be right down."

As he finished speaking, Lara appeared behind him. "Quick, everyone, eat fast!" she joked. "We may only have a few minutes before Monster-Baby wakes up."

It was a good ice-breaker. The parents in the crowd began recounting their tribulations with babies who wouldn't sleep or slept at the wrong times. No baby, it seemed, ever slept too much or too soundly.

Maxine directed everyone to their seats, taking care to separate couples. Mrs. Entwhistle looked around the table in amazement, wondering how Max could think so fast and direct so tactfully. *I would have had to draw a chart,* she thought, *and I still wouldn't have gotten it right.*

She sat at one end of the long table with Maxine at the other. Beside her, Marcie Devon enjoyed the courtly attention of Shyam, whose many years as proprietor of the Patel Paradise had made him expert at putting people at ease. Next to Maxine, Anna May and Chad exchanged uneasy small talk until Maxine asked Chad what was the worst thing and what was the best thing about his average day. It seemed a topic that kept on giving. Levi and Lara discovered they had a mutual interest in gardening, while Dex regaled Anjali and Adah with the story of Mrs. Entwhistle's eightieth birthday party.

"And then she and Maxine took off on the bike with the sidecar and I bet you could have heard them scream in the next county," Dex said, speaking into one of those inevitable lulls in the conversation so that everyone heard him, grinned and joined in.

"Remember, Roger rolled in manure and Booger was trying to give him a bath."

"And Roger got away, and Booger slipped and knocked all kinds of people over."

"It looked like rain, but then the day turned out beautifully."

"Maxine made that lovely cake."

Mrs. Entwhistle only half-listened. She'd been there, after all, and the whole day was etched in her memory. She tuned in to the low-voiced conversation between Marcie and Shyam on her right.

"Life is frequently not what we anticipate," Shyam said. "We make our choices in the light that we have at any given moment."

"But how does one ever know what to choose? And what if you fear you've chosen wrong?"

"Maybe then it is time for attributes other than choice to enter the equation," Shyam said. "For myself, I hope to always value loyalty and compassion. That is what Anjali demonstrated to me when I was quite ill, and she was left to carry the load."

Mrs. Entwhistle felt Roger settle down on her feet. Lured by the aromas from the table, he had forsaken his cushions, but clearly felt the need to rest. He sighed and settled his head on Mrs. Entwhistle's toes.

Anna May kept casting furtive glances at her brother and Adah. Her unease was apparent. Levi was having an animated conversation with Lara, but Adah sat silently, eyes down, paying attention only to her plate.

Mrs. Entwhistle hated for Anna May to have the extra emotional pressure of a disapproving sister-in-law this evening. The girl was still recovering from surgery and was alarmingly pale. Mrs. Entwhistle saw Anjali turn to Adah and ask a question, then another and another, until Adah finally had to respond or be overtly rude. She couldn't hear what was being said, but sent a silent blessing to Anjali for her tact.

After dinner, they all helped clear the table, and Mrs. Entwhistle and Maxine cleaned up the dishes and the kitchen with an economy of motion derived from many, many years of experience. Everyone gathered in the living room, seating themselves around the roaring fire that Shyam kept poking.

"Shyam, you do not want the chimney to catch fire," Anjali said quietly to her husband. "Maybe allow the fire to rest a bit?"

"Of course, Anjali," Shyam began, but paused and turned his head in the direction of the sound of an approaching motorcycle. Mrs. Entwhistle suddenly sat up straight and looked at the door. Anna May's eyes were wide. She rose and walked to the window, followed by Mrs. Entwhistle.

"That sounds like a Harley," Dex said, joining them at the window. "Anybody we know?"

"Why, yes, that's Joey," Mrs. Entwhistle said with an easiness she didn't feel. "Anna May, will you let him in?"

Anna May opened the door before Joey had a chance to ring the bell. She watched in amazement as he went down on one knee and extended a tiny black velvet box toward her. Oblivious of an audience, he had eyes only for Anna May.

"I love you," he said to her. "Will you marry me?"

.

Chapter Twenty-one

Mrs. Entwhistle felt Anna May sway and she put an arm around her waist. They stood together in silence contemplating the young man who knelt at their feet. Mrs. Entwhistle noticed icy pellets accumulating on the stoop.

Oh, no, not an ice storm! Not tonight. Nothing strxuck terror into Mrs. Entwhistle's Southern heart like an ice storm, but she stuffed down her fear. Somebody had to take charge of this ridiculously awkward moment.

"Joey, get up and come on in," she said. "Anna May needs to lie down for a little bit, but you come in and get warm. Let's get you something to eat and a hot drink. Why, look, there's a coating of ice on your helmet. Did you drive over icy roads?"

"Yes, ma'am," Joey said, slipping a little as he rose to his feet.

He put the velvet box in the pocket of his leather

jacket, a blush climbing up his neck, and stepped into the house. Mrs. Entwhistle handed Anna May off to Anjali, who escorted her firmly back to her bedroom.

"I'll introduce you to everyone later," Mrs. Entwhistle told Joey, "but for now, let's get you warm."

Joey was shivering, whether from nerves or cold she couldn't tell, but in either case, a hot cup of tea was called for. She gestured him to a seat at the kitchen table while she heated water and got out teabags.

"I don't really drink tea," Joey began, but Mrs. Entwhistle waved her hand.

"Tonight you do. How much sugar?"

"I don't use sugar."

"Tonight you do. It's good for stress. At least, that's what our English friends believe."

She set a steaming mug of tea and a plate of hastily assembled left-overs in front of Joey and sat down opposite. "Now. Tell me why you came. I mean, I guess I know, but tell me your thinking."

Joey sipped his tea and picked at the food for a minute before he answered. "I miss her," he finally said. "When I got home and found her gone and then saw your note, well, it just about killed me. I didn't realize how much I cared about her until she was gone."

Typical male, Mrs. Entwhistle thought with a mental snort. She nodded encouragingly for Joey to continue.

"At first, I figured she was faking being sick because she'd changed her mind about me and wanted an excuse to leave, so I got mad. I thought, okay, let her go if she wants to go. Then this morning my Dad told me he'd heard from someone he knows in this town. Well, from a girlfriend, actually. She said Anna May had an operation and had been in the hospital. I got right on the bike and came after her."

"You just happened to have an engagement ring handy?" Mrs. Entwhistle couldn't help asking. She liked for all i's to be dotted and all t's crossed.

"I got it from my Dad. He was going to give it to his girlfriend, but he changed his mind. I swiped it."

"Hmmm. So coming here was an impulsive decision involving theft," she said. "Doesn't seem like the best thinking."

"Yeah, you're right. Anna May looked at me like I was nuts."

"You probably are. People in love tend to be."

"Do you... do you think I might have a chance with her?"

"I think you have a better chance of getting your nose punched by her brother. He's in the living room right now," Mrs. Entwhistle said, unconsciously touching the eye where she'd taken her own punch.

"Oh, yeah? Well, let him come on, then," Joey said, balling his hands into fists.

"Stop it. This is Christmas Eve. If we are iced in together on the holiest night of the year, I can assure you that manners will be observed." Mrs. Entwhistle's Mom-glare could have stopped a train, let alone a tired, cold, heart-sick boy. "You'll be sleeping on the sofa because all the rooms are full. I expect you to be on your best behavior, and Levi, too. Now. Come along and say hello to the other guests."

Joey followed Mrs. Entwhistle into the living room and nodded dazedly at all the names that flew around his head. Then he headed straight for Levi. "Could I talk to you privately for a minute?" he asked.

The young men stepped outside. Ignoring the icy rain, Joey extended his hand to Levi.

"I owe you an apology," he said, "for taking Anna May away from you and your folks. It would have been better if all of us had talked things out right then and there."

"I got nothing to say to you," Levi said, ignoring Joey's outstretched hand. "Far as I'm concerned, you're nothing but a carnie drifter who ruined my sister."

Joey took a deep breath and swallowed hard. "Okay. I just want to say that I really care for Anna May and want her to have a good life. I hope that'll be with me, but if she thinks different, I won't make a fuss."

"If you know her at all," Levi said, "you know she makes her own decisions. If she decides to be with you, do you have any idea what you'd be getting into? Say she comes back home and stays Amish and brings you with her. Are you willing to give up the life you know? You'd never really be accepted no matter how hard you tried. Oh, everyone would be polite to you for Anna May's sake, but you'd never belong. People don't become Amish; you're either born to it or you're not. We don't go looking for converts."

"Fair enough," Joey said. "I appreciate your honesty."

"And if she decides to stay here and be English, she'll kiss her family goodbye. I'll stick by her, but our folks and her other brothers and sisters will have nothing to do with her. There won't be financial help or inheritance, if that's what you're after."

"It's not," Joey said, again swallowing his anger at Levi's insults. Much as he resented the other man's frankness, he needed the information Levi was imparting. "Anna May is all I want, if she'll have me."

"Well, that's up to her. I hope she won't. Just so you know."

"Got it."

They stepped back into the warm house, each feeling bruised by their conversation, but somehow relieved, too. All the cards were on the table.

~*~

Mrs. Entwhistle and Maxine were having an urgent conference in the kitchen. "It's sleeting out there," Mrs. Entwhistle said, nodding her head toward the window. "You know what that means."

"Do I ever. Power failure, trees crashing down, car accidents. I just hope the electricity stays on." But as Maxine spoke there was an ominous flicker of the lights.

"Let's get ready, just in case." Mrs. Entwhistle sat down with a paper and pencil and began a list. "Do you have candles and flashlights? What about old kerosene lanterns? Extra blankets and comforters for the beds? Firewood?"

"I've got two boxes of candles and there's a flashlight with new batteries in every room. I don't think there are any old kerosene lanterns still around, but I've got two camping lanterns. Firewood, yes, there's plenty, but it's out in the shed."

"We've got some strong young men who can carry it in. There's a fireplace in each bedroom, so if worse comes to worst, we can at least take the chill off. It won't be cozy, but no one will freeze, either. Luckily, you've got a gas range and water heater, so we can cook and take hot showers."

"We'll *have* to cook; the refrigerator and freezer are chock-full. If the power goes off for any length of time, that food will need to be prepared before it spoils," Maxine said.

"You're in luck, then; there are some wonderful cooks right here in the house. But it probably won't come to that. The only good thing about a Southern ice storm is it usually doesn't last very long. If we can keep everybody comfortable for twenty-four hours, the ice will have melted and the crews will be out fixing the power outages."

"I'm worried about that big old pine that leans over the west side of the house. What if it crashes? I should have had that tree taken down last summer, but there were so many expenses I decided to put it off until later. Oh, why was I so stupid?"

"Now, none of that," Mrs. Entwhistle said firmly. "If we could foretell the future, we'd be in business with Madam Esmeralda."

"I hope Esmeralda's safe in this storm," Maxine said.

"If she's not, it's her own fault. She should have seen it coming," Mrs. Entwhistle said callously.

The wind picked up, whistling around the corners of the house. They exchanged apprehensive glances. Mrs. Entwistle got to her feet and walked into the living room.

"Levi, Dex, Joey and Chad," she said. "We've got some bad weather brewing. I need you to carry in enough firewood to see us through the night in case we lose power. The furnace in this house is gas-powered, but the fan that pushes the heat through the ducts runs on electricity. If we lose power it's going to get cold in here. We're fortunate to have a number of fireplaces to take the chill off, and Maxine is well-stocked with firewood, but we need it carried inside."

The men immediately stood and fetched their coats, all except for Chad. "Um, I don't have anything but my overcoat. It's cashmere. I'd hate to snag it on firewood."

"No problem," Mrs. Entwhistle said. She opened the basement door and took a particularly nasty parka from a hook in the stairwell. "Here you go."

Chad eyed it dubiously. Maxine's husband had worn that parka for any chore that came to mind, and a few that didn't. It still carried the odors of animals both wild and domestic, cheap cigar smoke and a musky sort of sweat.

"I think it's waterproof," Mrs. Entwhistle said helpfully, thrusting the garment at Chad again.

He took it between thumb and forefinger the way he might take a dead rat if someone offered it.

"And my shoes," he said. "I didn't bring boots."

They both looked down at Chad's deeply-shined cordovan tasseled loafers. Mrs. Entwhistle didn't know much about expensive shoes, but she knew 'em when she saw 'em. She didn't blame Chad for not wanting to ruin this pair.

"Easy fix." She fetched two plastic grocery bags and two stout rubber bands. "Put the bags over your shoes and fasten them around your ankles with the elastic bands. You wouldn't want to run a marathon, but they'll work for a while. I used to do this for my kids in bad weather. It's not really worth it to buy snow boots in this climate. Here, you can carry the flashlight."

Poor man, she thought, watching Chad plod after the others, the little round circle of the light drooping in front of him. He didn't come prepared to rough it. She smiled at the memory of his pinched nostrils when he donned the parka. It had been hanging on that hook since Maxine's husband passed. Max claimed she couldn't bear to wash it, and Mrs. Entwhistle believed her, but suspected her reluctance had more to do with repugnance than grief.

The men made several trips to and fro with armloads of firewood, which they dumped near each fireplace. "How many fireplaces are there?" Dex inquired, breathing hard after his third trip up the stairs.

"One in every room, just about. This house was built before central heating," Maxine said. "The ones in the bedrooms haven't been used for ages. I'm afraid to think what will happen if we light fires in them."

"Well, maybe it won't be necessary," Mrs. Entwhistle said. "Let's get some pails of water ready."

"What for?" Dex asked.

"Flushing," Mrs. Entwhistle said succinctly.

Her mind retraced steps taken in earlier ice storms. They'd need drinking water, so she proceeded to fill every pitcher and carafe she could find. They'd need snacks; people who were house-bound always ate a lot, she'd learned. So she popped corn, washed apples and set out peanut butter and crackers.

As Mrs. Entwhistle was finishing her preparations, the lights suddenly went out. There was no warning flicker, just an instantaneous descent into darkness.

The refrigerator motor went silent in mid-hum, the dishwasher groaned to a stop, and the only clock still keeping time was the old grandfather in the hall. The women in the living room reacted with little screams of dismay. They still had firelight, but the back of the house was dark. Mrs. Entwhistle hurried to light a candle.

"And even though I've lighted a candle, I still intend to curse the darkness," she said to Dex as he staggered in with a big armload of wood.

"Huh?" he replied, too preoccupied to field her literary reference. "Where do you want this?"

"Upstairs, and while you're up there, check on Thomas. Make sure he has enough covers."

"Babies aren't allowed covers anymore," Dex said. "We aren't supposed to use any blankets or sheets or pillows or bumper pads in his crib. He has to sleep on his back in just a warm sleeper."

"Well, my land!" Mrs. Entwhistle exclaimed. "The poor little scrap will freeze to death in an unheated house."

"I'll check with Lara," Dex said, heading up the stairs. "She'll know what to do."

Mrs. Entwhistle remembered when her pediatrician was equally adamant about having bumper pads around the inside of the crib so babies wouldn't get their heads stuck between the bars. And all infants were put to sleep on their tummies, requiring a feat of dexterity to flip them over in mid-air as they were lowered into their cribs. Every generation of conscientious parents tried to do the right thing, but in her experience, the rules kept changing.

Levi and Joey entered the back door, laughing about something, their earlier animosity evaporating in the shared emergency.

"This is one time when we Amish have the advantage," Levi was saying. "We know how to get along without electricity."

Chad trailed in the door, a couple of pieces of firewood in one hand, the flashlight in the other. He looked so forlorn in his stinky borrowed coat and tattered grocery bag boots that Mrs. Entwhistle laughed out loud.

She clapped him on the back, raising a little puff of dust. "Chad, you're a champ. Come have some hot chocolate after you've delivered your kindling."

Chapter Twenty-two

Marcie gave herself silent kudos for bringing her warmest sweater. She'd packed it automatically, not stopping to think that she was going to a more temperate climate. Now, with the temperature dropping and ice pellets tapping at the windows, she was glad to have it. Despite being marooned by bad weather in a houseful of strangers, she felt a flicker of happiness. The Inn was beautiful and comfortable, and somehow Chad seemed less annoying now than he did at home. This trip was turning out to be an adventure.

Her good mood went out with the lights.

"Chad?" she called into the darkness of their bedroom, which was stupid because she knew he was outside with the other men. "Chad?" she called again, hearing the rising note in her own voice.

Marcie remembered seeing a flashlight in the

drawer of the bedside table when she'd been reconnoitering the room, and she felt her way there and grabbed it. The light was strong and bright. Unfortunately, the mirror caught its reflection and gave her back a picture of herself that was the scariest thing of all.

When did I get to be an old hag? Who is that woman with the hollow cheeks and the black under-eye circles? Surely that can't be me?

But it was. Before she could collect herself, the bedroom door opened and Chad entered with an armload of firewood. Marcie shone the flashlight over her husband, taking in the greasy parka and grocery bag booties. In spite of herself, she began to laugh.

"Oh, Chad, aren't we a pair? Look at us, enjoying our Christmas getaway!"

"What's so darn funny?"

He took a good look at his wife, bundled up in her expensive sweater, white-faced and big-eyed, and then glanced down at himself. "Okay, it is kind of funny," he admitted. "We're definitely not the same couple who left home."

"Can you build a fire?"

"I don't know; are we supposed to? Or should we wait...?"

"Oh, come on, let's walk on the wild side," Marcie said, still laughing.

Somehow the dark, rapidly cooling house released

something mischievous in her. She knelt and began stacking the wood in the grate. They'd never owned a fireplace, but Marcie remembered seeing her father build fires.

"We should have rolled up newspapers or something, I think," she said. "But let's just see if it will catch. Do you have a match?"

"Why would I? You know I don't smoke."

"Okay, wait a minute, I picked up a matchbook in that place we stopped for coffee. Let me see if I can find it."

Marcie rummaged through her purse, feeling for the little book of matches. When she finally found it, she struck match after match only to watch the tiny flame die before she could coax a response from a log.

"Here, let me try," Chad said, kneeling at her side in a manly fashion.

He took the parchment paper menu Maxine had left in each room, crumpled it, stuffed it between two pieces of wood and held a match to one corner. The paper lit up with a crackle, and the nearest log began smoldering. They coughed as smoke billowed into the room.

"Were we supposed to open a damper or something?" Marcie choked out, waving her hand in front of her nose.

The smoke detector chose that moment to do its duty, filling the room with shrill shrieks. Marcie's alarmed eyes met Chad's as Mrs. Entwhistle burst through the door brandishing a fire extinguisher.

"Everyone stand back," she roared, aiming blindly in the dark room. She pulled the trigger and a cloud of white fire retardant shot forth, covering Chad and Marcie where they knelt on the hearth. They scrambled backwards on their heels, yelling, "No, stop, you're spraying us!"

Mrs. Entwhistle advanced into the room, her eyes adjusting to the ambient light.

"Oh, wait, it's just the fireplace smoking," she said in a more normal tone. "Oopsy."

She stepped into the bathroom, filled a paper cup with water and doused the smoldering log. Then she opened a window and turned on the ceiling fan. The temperature dropped, but at least they could breathe without coughing. The Devons scraped the retardant off their faces with the sides of their fingers, blinking at her like two wet owls.

"Sorry about that," Mrs. Entwhistle said. "I thought something was on fire, and I guess I got carried away. Are you okay?"

"I think so," Chad said. He sneezed violently three times in a row.

"Maxine was just saying she didn't know what would happen if we tried to light fires in these bedroom fireplaces," Mrs. Entwhistle said. "I bet you forgot to open the damper. Sorry about spraying you. You'd better wash all that stuff off and change your clothes. I hope it won't stain."

Marcie glanced down at her expensive sweater ruefully. "No problem," she said.

Chad looked at her in surprise. Marcie had been known to fling a fit over lesser affronts than this.

"Come on downstairs after you get cleaned up," Mrs. Entwhistle said. "Everyone is gathered around the living room fireplace, which is drawing just fine. We've got candles and board games and snacks. Oh, and there's no need to tell everyone what happened up here, you know, about dampers and fire extinguishers and such. We'll just say the smoke detector went off by mistake and everything's been taken care of."

Mrs. Entwhistle nodded brightly at the two retardant-drenched guests as if getting smoked and sprayed were a normal part of the Amish Inn experience. She wasn't eager to expose herself to the teasing she knew would be forthcoming if Dex learned of her little misfire.

Levi and Adah weren't on the best of terms considering they were newly-weds.

"It ain't right that we're here," Adah said for the fourth time. "We don't belong with these English."

"They're just people, like anybody," Levi said.

"Not like us," Adah said, her bottom lip stuck out. "They look at us like we're carnival freaks or something."

"That ought to make Joey feel right at home," Levi

said, but Adah didn't smile.

"Yah, and what about him? Just think what your folks would say if he and Anna May, well, I don't even know what you'd call it. Hook up? Shack up? I guess they've already done that."

Levi hated to hear the judgmental tone in his new wife's voice. "We just have to trust that Ammay will make the right decision," he said. "And, Adah, I told you before we got married: Anna May is my sister and I'm going to stay on good terms with her no matter what she does. You knew that."

"Yes, Levi," Adah said submissively, but she had to look down to hide the rebellion in her eyes.

Levi's lips compressed, but he decided he didn't want to argue with Adah right now. She'd never been this far from her father's farm, and they were in an unfamiliar house filled with strangers. It was enough to make anyone uneasy. He'd cut her some slack.

~*~

Dex and Lara were tiptoeing around their dark room, trying not to wake Thomas. They glanced fearfully at their sleeping son every time a floorboard squeaked or a window rattled. Dex shielded the candle flame with one hand as Lara dug through their suitcase to find their extra sweaters.

"Do you think he'll sleep through until morning?" Lara whispered.

"God only knows. Night before last, he woke at four

and never went back to sleep, remember?"

"Oh, yeah, I remember."

They grinned at each other. Parenthood was a lot tougher than they'd imagined, but it was fun, too. Dex thought it was like being on a lifeboat together, trying to negotiate unfamiliar seas. His love and respect for his wife grew as he saw her transform into a mother before his eyes. She said she'd never loved Dex more than the first time he'd changed a loaded diaper.

They were still young enough to view adversity as adventure.

Joey and Anna May sat silently in the living room, staring at the fire. The beautiful Christmas tree lights had gone out when the power failed, but the firelight more than made up for it. Even Anna May's tired face took on a rosy glow.

"Is it all right with you if I stay the night, like Mrs. Entwhistle said," Joey asked shyly.

"I don't think you have much choice," Anna May said. "The roads are dangerous, and nothing else is open tonight." She paused, then asked, "What did you think was going to happen when you got here? Did you think I'd fall into your arms and you'd carry me off on the back of your bike like you did before?"

"I didn't stop to make a plan. When I heard you'd been so sick, I just came."

Anna May sighed. "That's really nice of you."

"Yeah, but I think maybe you'd rather I wasn't here."

"It makes things more complicated, and I'm so tired. It's hard to deal with everything."

'Look, no pressure from me, okay? Forget about that proposal. I don't know what I was thinking, surprising you like that. You don't need to make any decisions. Just rest and get better. Everything will work itself out." He held out his hand.

After a moment, Anna May took it. They sat like that, holding hands, looking into the fire. After a bit, Anna May rested her head on Joey's shoulder.

~*~

Shyam and Anjali Patel were having a conference with Maxine and Mrs. Entwhistle. They'd planned to sleep in their own home and return early in the morning to make breakfast for the guests. Now that didn't seem feasible.

"All the bedrooms are full," Shyam said. "But we can sit up. It would not be the first time."

"No, you must take the bedroom Max and I were going to share," Mrs. Entwhistle said. "I'll be perfectly comfortable on one of the recliners in the study, and besides, it will be easier with Roger. Sometimes he needs to go out in the middle of the night."

"And I'll take the other recliner," Max said. "Joey will be on the sofa in the living room. What we need to do is get all the extra blankets and pillows we can find. The house will cool down fast and the fireplaces can't heat the whole house."

Mrs. Entwhistle remembered the state of one of those fireplaces. She said, "We ought to build the fires ourselves. People might forget to, uh, open the damper or something."

Mrs. Entwhistle and Shyam declared themselves the fire-starting team. Maxine and Anjali went to round up extra bedding. Mrs. Entwhistle felt her legs protesting what seemed like the umpteenth trip up the long staircase. She was thankful she didn't have to tote an armful of logs. They did carry plenty of newspapers with them, and long kitchen matches. When all the fires were laid, lit and determined to be non-smoking, she and Shyam returned to the relative warmth of the kitchen. The gas oven was on with the door open, taking the chill off the room. On the stovetop, teakettles simmered with hot water, ready to make cups of hot chocolate and tea. Plates of cookies and nuts were on the table. They wouldn't starve and they wouldn't freeze, not tonight.

They heard the sound of footsteps on the stairs. Their guests were gathering.

Chapter Twenty-three

"So, who's up for some sledding?" Dex asked, rubbing his hands. "There's a good coating of ice all over the road and that slope in front of the house is calling. I found an old sled in the garage when we were gathering firewood. Who's game?"

Levi shook his head no. He wouldn't leave Adah alone, and he knew she'd never unbend enough to go sledding with this group. Joey also said no because Anna May wasn't well enough to participate. Maxine said she'd stay in and listen for Thomas, in case he woke. Marcie was surprised to see Chad jump to his feet enthusiastically.

"I'll go," he said. He fetched the awful parka and grocery bag boots.

Marcie got to her feet, too, in solidarity. "Count me in," she said.

"Sounds like fun," Mrs. Entwhistle said. "I think I'll

join you."

All heads swiveled in her direction.

"Uh, do you think it's wise, I mean, you are eighty," Dex's voice dried up under Mrs. Entwhistle's withering glare. "Uh, a very lively and vigorous eighty, too."

But it was too late, and Dex knew it. If there was any way to absolutely ensure that Mrs. Entwhistle would do something, it was to hint that she shouldn't because she was too old.

"I was sledding before y'all were even twinkles in your daddies' eyes," she said, getting into her coat, hat, boots and gloves. "Why do young people think fun cuts off at a certain age?"

Ignoring the horrified glances, Mrs. Entwhistle joined the sledding party as they made their way with some difficulty to the top of the hill. The street was already full of children sliding on anything from cookie sheets to snow saucers. Southerners were never prepared for icy conditions, but they didn't let that stop them. Winter sports opportunities were rare and they were going to enjoy this one by any means possible.

Dex politely turned the sled over to Marcie and Chad. "You go first, you're actual paying guests," he said.

They settled themselves, Marcie sitting between Chad's legs. Dex gave them a shove and they were off. They'd been skiing in the Swiss Alps, ice-skating in Rockefeller Center, and bob-sledding in Austria, but they whooped in glee just like the kids all around them.

Mrs. Entwhistle and Dex were next. "But I want to go alone," Mrs. Entwhistle said. "I remember how to do this." She was still a little mad at him. "And give me a good send-off, not a wimpy one."

Settling herself well back on the sled, she waved a hand and Dex gave her a push that rocked her head back.

She was flying! It seemed she was traveling faster than when she rode her scooter. The other sledders flashed past in a blur. She yanked at the steering rope, but it was old and rotten and broke off in her hand. In vain, she leaned to the left and to the right, steering tricks she remembered from her youth, but the sled was heedless.

The pond at the bottom of the street was an unassuming little body of water. Toddlers splashed in it. Children fished in it. In the heat of the summer, the pond dried up completely, but at the moment it was full of autumn rain. Mrs. Entwhistle knew that soon it would be full of her, too.

In desperation, she closed her eyes and rolled off the sled onto the icy ground. She kept sliding, but felt herself slowing. When she opened her eyes, she was at the bottom of the hill looking up at a circle of silent, staring children.

"Are you okay?" one of them asked, more in curiosity than concern.

Before she knew what to say, she felt Dex's strong

arms lifting her and steadying her on the icy road. Before them, the sled rocked gently in the waters of the pond.

"Oh, my gosh, that could be you out there," Dex said in a shaky voice. "I shouldn't have let you go alone. Do you think you're okay? Anything hurt?"

"Only my pride," Mrs. Entwhistle confessed. She felt Dex's body sag in relief. "Besides, I wouldn't have drowned, just gotten soaked. Why do you think I went so fast?"

"Power-to-weight ratio is equal to thrust per unit mass multiplied by the velocity of any vehicle," Dex intoned, giving up his struggle not to laugh.

"Oh, shut up," Mrs. Entwhistle said, punching him on the arm. "I'll give you power-to-weight ratio!"

The story of her sled ride continued to grow in depth and breadth as it was repeated to the occupants of the Amish Inn in the flickering candle light.

"And I never did get a turn," Dex finished. "The sled is at the bottom of the pond by now. You'll find it next summer. It'll be a reminder of the Amish Inn ice storm."

Mrs. Entwhistle didn't think she'd need any reminders. She was starting to ache in places she didn't even know were places. A hot bath and her own bed, those were the things she longed for and knew she wouldn't be getting, not that night. Maxine set a glass of water and a bottle of aspirin in front of her without a hint of reproach. Mrs. Entwhistle thought again there never was a better friend than Max.

Marcie and Chad privately agreed that they had to give the old lady points for grit. Not only did she go sledding at her age, she took her fall good-humoredly.

"I hope I'm like that when I'm her age," Marcie whispered in Chad's ear. Her breath tickled; it reminded him of when they were courting and had so many confidential things to say to each other.

"You're already a fearless woman," Chad whispered back. "And a beautiful one."

It had been a long time since Marcie had received a compliment from her husband, and she actually blushed. That made Chad laugh and lean over and kiss her. They gazed into each other's eyes.

"Hot chocolate?" Mrs. Entwhistle inquired, waving the pot in front of them.

"Um, no, thanks. I think we'll just turn in for the night," Chad replied, not breaking eye contact with his wife. Suddenly, he couldn't wait to get her alone in their bedroom, the room with the fire burning cleanly in the grate and the faint smell of retardant foam in the air. The Amish Inn was exceeding his expectations so far, and the night was young.

~*~

The last thing anyone expected was a visitor, so they all jumped when they heard the doorbell. Anna May answered, candle in hand, and reappeared in the kitchen.

"It's a man who says his name is Bagel," she reported. "Or Burglar? Should I let him in?"

"Oh, yes, that's just Booger; he's an old friend," Mrs. Entwhistle said.

Booger, in the meanwhile, had let himself in, shucked off his boots inside the door and now appeared wearing his fur cap with the ear flaps and his enormous red mittens. He skidded slightly in his sock feet, and Mrs. Entwhistle noted that his big toe poked through the left one.

Booger's son, Caleb, followed, carrying a large cardboard box.

"Hi-dy, y'all," Caleb said. "We brung you some supplies."

"How did you get here on the ice?" Maxine asked.

"I got chains for the truck," Booger said. "This ain't my first ice storm. We brung some canned goods, in case you was caught short with all the people here."

Mrs. Entwhistle side-eyed Maxine. They knew Booger's canned goods were millennia past their sell-by date.

"Why, Booger, that's just so nice of you. We're much obliged," Maxine caroled. "Now you and Caleb sit down and have some hot chocolate and cookies."

Both men accepted the invitation promptly. Maxine cringed a little to see the rapid decimation of her carefully iced Christmas cookies.

"It's Christmas," Mrs. Entwhistle whispered. "That's what we made 'em for."

Maxine nodded and refilled the plate. Anjali poured more hot chocolate and Sanjay sat down beside Booger for a serious talk about frozen pipes and how long food could last in a powerless refrigerator. Since the two men had gone into the tiny-house development business, Shyam looked to Booger as the fount of all knowledge.

Anna May and Joey appeared in the kitchen doorway. "Did we hear that you took a fall?" Anna May asked Mrs. Entwhistle.

"She took more of a splash-down than a fall," Dex explained helpfully. "I've never seen anybody move so fast without the power of a gasoline engine. You should have been there..." His voice trailed off as he escorted the two of them back into the living room. Mrs. Entwhistle heard the laughter.

"Well, I'm glad I can still amuse the young," she muttered.

~*~

It wasn't the most restful night Mrs. Entwhistle had ever spent. She and Maxine laid back the old leather recliners as far as they would go, piled on the quilts and comforters and settled in for the night. Mrs. Entwhistle held Roger in her lap under the covers. The old dog suffered from the cold and she wanted to make sure he slept warm that night.

In a way, it was like the old days when she and Max had had slumber parties. They talked and giggled now just as they had long ago.

"What do you think happened to Marcie and Chad?" Maxine asked. "They didn't seem to be on very good terms when they arrived, but now, oo la la!"

"Sledding seems to have surprising outcomes for some of us," Mrs. Entwhistle replied, shifting uncomfortably. Her back had stiffened up since her fall, and she had a feeling she'd need her cane tomorrow.

"What about Anna May and Joey? Do you think she'll go away with him?"

Mrs. Entwhistle shrugged. "I don't know what to predict there. Anna May has been through a lot, and it's bound to affect her judgment. I'm glad Levi is here to be a steadying influence for her, but that wife of his!"

"Ah, yes, Adah. She seems a bit tightly wound." Maxine would never say anything very bad about anybody.

"Yes, that's a good way to put it," Mrs. Entwhistle agreed. "I hope she can relax a little before they go home. Say, when *are* they going home?"

"I don't think they said." Maxine yawned widely.

They both lay their heads back and fell silent. Tomorrow was Christmas Day, and they needed to be rested. Roger snored like a furry metronome. Soon Mrs. Entwhistle's breathing matched his. They slept.

They didn't hear the outraged cries of young

Thomas Schofield, or the quiet footsteps of his father as Dex as he tiptoed to the kitchen and made Lara a warming cup of tea to drink while she nursed their baby. Mrs. Entwhistle snored gently as Joey made his way from the sofa to Anna May's bedroom and knocked softly. They didn't hear her say, "No, Joey." Maxine sighed and burrowed deeper into the covers when the front door latch clicked shut. The motorcycle coasting down the icy street didn't disturb them, nor the chimes of the old grandfather clock in the hall.

"Why, I don't think I slept a wink," Mrs. Entwhistle said when she stirred at six.

Maxine was already up, trailing a blanket wrapped around her shoulders. She handed Mrs. Entwhistle a cup of English Breakfast tea with two sugars, then settled down with her own cup. From the kitchen came wonderful aromas.

"Are Shyam and Anjali making Belgian waffles?" Mrs. Entwhistle asked, sniffing appreciatively.

"Yes, and bacon and eggs and sausages and freshly-squeezed orange juice and, of course, my cinnamon rolls," Maxine said. "What luxury, to have someone else doing the cooking. I could lie here all day."

But Roger couldn't, and he soon poked his nose out of the blankets and gave Mrs. Entwhistle an urgent stare. He needed to go out.

With that, the day began. The power crews worked diligently in the bright morning sunshine and by eight o'clock electricity was restored. The last glittering ice crystals would be melted even in the shady spots by noon. The Christmas tree lights came to life and all the digital clocks, blinking on twelve o'clock, started over. With no regrets for time lost, they began counting out the seconds, minutes and hours again. Mrs. Entwhistle thought there was a life lesson somewhere in that.

Chapter Twenty-four

Marcie and Chad wandered into the dining room hand-in-hand. They didn't say much, but the aura of young love clung to them like a cloud.

Mrs. Entwhistle appreciated romance as much as the next person. She smiled as she poured their coffee and offered a basket of cinnamon rolls fresh from the oven.

"Merry Christmas! Did you sleep well?" she asked innocently. "I hope you weren't too chilly."

"Oh, no," Marcie said, exchanging a very private look with Chad. "We were warm enough. The fire in our room never went out."

I'll bet, Mrs. Entwhistle thought, but she only nodded. "That's good, then. The power is back on and the house will be warm soon. You can shower and get yourselves together. It will be a quiet Christmas, but the newspaper carrier got through so there are newspapers to read, and there's a carol service at the church you may want to take in. And it's a lovely day for a walk. Tomorrow you'll be on your way back home."

"Actually, we aren't going home," Chad said. "Not just yet."

Mrs. Entwhistle's ears pricked up apprehensively. She knew Maxine was definitely not prepared to have the Inn's soft opening extend beyond today.

Chad continued. "We're going to Paris. That's where we honeymooned, and we, well, we feel like going back."

"Just like that? Do you even have your passports with you?" Mrs. Entwhistle was intrigued by such an impulsive decision taken by these two rather starchy young people.

"Oh, we always have our passports with us," Chad said. "We'll drive to the airport in Atlanta and book the first flight we can get."

Mrs. Entwhistle took that in. "What about your jobs?"

"I've got all kinds of work commitments, but for once, I'm going to put Chad first," Marcie said. "They can get along without me at work, but I don't think I can get along without Chad."

Mrs. Entwhistle smiled agreeably, but the atmosphere was getting a little too thick with pheromones to suit her. She left the coffee pot and the rolls and returned to the kitchen.

"Whew, for a minute there I thought Chad and Marcie were going to ask to stay another day," she said to Maxine. "But no, they're off to Paris."

"Paris! How romantic!" Maxine loved a happy ending. "Do you think their stay here at the Inn had anything to do with that decision?"

"Of course. This is a regular love nest. Maybe we should rename it the Hormone Inn."

Adah laced up her black shoes, pulled the shoestrings tight and tied double knots. She looked as neat as a pin, and almost as sharp. Levi shrugged into his homemade black jacket and zipped the duffel bag closed.

"What about Anna May?" Adah asked. "What's she going to do?"

"Well, she ain't going with Joey, because he's already gone."

"He left? When?"

"During the night, I guess. Mrs. Entwhistle said he was gone when she got up. He must have had second thoughts and decided to make himself scarce. Don't know how he could ride that motorcycle on icy roads."

"He's a very changeable person," Adah said with a disapproving sniff. "Anna May is better off without him. He's not our kind. What's she going to do, stay here or go home with us?"

"I don't know. I didn't ask and she didn't say."

"Well, I want to go home. I've got a lot to do to get our house in order. I don't want to wait around while your sister makes up her mind."

"I know; we're going. I've hired a driver to take us to the bus station. Just let me go down and talk to Anna May one more time before we leave."

He found her in the kitchen. She followed him when he inclined his head toward her bedroom. Once inside, Levi shut the door and motioned for Anna May to sit down on the bed. He sat beside her. Theirs was not an openly affectionate family, but he took her cold hand in his warm one.

"Ammay, do you know what you're going to do? Have you made your decision?"

She looked down, biting her lip. Then she raised her eyes to his and said, "I'm staying, Levi. I know it's going to hurt Mom and Pop and all of you, and I'm so sorry. Do you think they will shun me?"

Levi returned her gaze steadily. "Not officially. You're not a church member, so you won't be placed under the miting, but Mom says you can't come home if you go high. Pop will go along with whatever she says. You have to know you are giving them up."

Anna May cried then, and Levi patted her back like she was a very little sister. When she'd cried herself out, she blew her nose, wiped her eyes and set her chin. "I hate it. I just hate it, but my decision stands. I'll miss everyone so much, but maybe, in time, they'll relent. Even if they don't, I have to do what I think is right for me."

"What *is* right for you? Have you decided?"

"I'm going to stay here and run the Inn for Maxine. Joey, well, I don't know what will happen with him. I have a lot to do before I'll be ready for any kind of relationship. I want to finish high school and then go on to college. Delilah says I can do most of it online, and she'll help me. I don't know what I want to do with my life yet, but I'll find out as I go along. Maybe I'll be a writer. I could tell the story of what it means to be Amish, and what it means to leave. But I'll have to have more life experiences before I'm wise enough to do that." She gripped Levi's hand again. "Do you understand? Can you forgive me?"

"Nothing to forgive, sis. You'll always be welcome at my house."

"Really? Do you think Adah would agree?"

"We'll be working on it," Levi said, smiling. "I guess we need to have more life experiences, too, but we'll figure things out. You just remember you're not alone. You have a brother. And if you ever need it, you have a home."

~*~

Dex and Laura decided to stay another couple of days.

"But not here," Mrs. Entwhistle hurried to reassure Maxine. "They're coming home with me. Truth to tell, I think Dex misses our little town. He wants to talk to Jimmy Jack down at the paper and swap newspaper stories. He wants to eat beef and noodles at the Busy Bee Diner and see your new house and the tiny house community. And I intend to shoo Lara out to get a pedicure and a haircut while I take care of Thomas. She admitted she's feeling raggedy and could use a little time off."

"Don't I remember!" Maxine said. Her daughter was a grown woman, but the memory of those exhausting early days of motherhood never faded. "They could stay on here, though. It wouldn't be any trouble."

"No, Max, you've got a schedule for opening the Inn and you should stick to it. You've learned a lot from this informal opening; don't allow yourself to get rushed. Besides, I want the Schofields all to myself!"

"Well, not *all* to yourself. I'm going to get my hands on that baby," Maxine said. "And I'll make soup for supper one night."

"Potato?"

"Sure, if that's what you want. And peach cobbler, with the peaches I put up last summer."

"Okay, then. I guess I'll let you come over."

"As if you could stop me."

~*~

Shyam and Anjali unlocked the front door of their tiny house and entered apprehensively. Had the pipes burst? Had the contents of the refrigerator spoiled during the power outage? A quick investigation proved that neither of those things had happened, and they took a deep breath in relief.

"Just one night away, and I could not wait to get back to our place," Anjali said.

The tiny house had been Shyam's idea when it proved impossible for them to continue their travels. He sometimes worried that their life was structured to suit him, not Anjali. He wanted his wife to be happy, too. His eyes followed her anxiously as she moved about the small room, touching surfaces, straightening cushions, smoothing a curtain back into place.

"Does it feel like home to you?" Shyam asked.

"Shyam, of course it feels like home," Anjali said, shaking her head and smiling at his worry. "Did I not choose every finish? Did I not sew the curtains and select the furniture? It is our little cottage, and we are so lucky to have it and each other. Our son is settled and happy; he and his family are nearby. What more could I want?"

Roger was happy to get back to his familiar haunts. The temperature had risen to a comfortable level, so Mrs. Entwhistle removed his itchy Christmas sweater and let him out to re-explore the back yard. The fearsome tomcat next door wasn't in evidence, so Roger could take his time checking out the latest depredations of the squirrels. They'd been in the bird feeder again. He sniffed at the scattered seeds on the ground and sneezed explosively.

Later, he'd have his supper in his good old supper

dish, and then he'd signal Mrs. Entwhistle to lift him up on the sofa. He couldn't reliably leap there anymore, but she always seemed to know what he wanted. His favorite cushions were waiting. They smelled just right and molded to his shape exactly. He'd have a peaceful pre-bedtime nap, then a long, satisfying night full of doggie dreams at the foot of Mrs. Entwhistle's bed.

Roger wasn't a particularly wise little dog. If he'd had the gift of speech he wouldn't have had anything stunning to say, but sometimes words weren't needed. Roger lifted his old head and curled his feathery tail over his back to express his satisfaction with life. He knew the best journey takes you home.

~End~

ABOUT THE AUTHOR

Doris Reidy is the author of six Mrs. Entwhistle books and four other works of fiction. She began writing novels and short stories at the age of 70, after a free-lance career that included articles in newspapers and magazines. Her Hoosier roots were transplanted in Marietta, Georgia in 1974, and she reports that the natives have almost stopped asking her why she talks funny. The Mrs. Entwhistle series follows the adventures of Cora Entwhistle, a formidable lady of a certain age who still has a lot of living to do. Doris adamantly denies that Mrs. E. is based on herself. "I barely know her," she protests. "But I like her."

Doris Reidy

Made in the USA
Las Vegas, NV
10 November 2022

59172982R00153